The Critics Cheer
MURDER OFF THE GLASS

"A NOVEL WITH PERSONALITY, HUMOR . . . and as much bounce as a dribbling exhibition. A fine first mystery with a smiling face."
>—Richard Rosen,
>author of *Strike Three You're Dead* and *Fadeaway*

"A COMIC MYSTERY IN THE DONALD WEST-LAKE TRADITION . . . The atmosphere is perfect. . . . *Murder off the Glass* is like an off-balance jump shot that rolls tantalizingly around the rim before dropping through for the score."
>—*Chicago Sun-Times*

"A HIGHLY ENTERTAINING TALE. Katz displays a flair for witty dialogue and for funny characters as well. Basketball may be an unusual milieu for a detective story, but the tale rings true."
>—*Publishers Weekly*

"AN AMUSING FIRST NOVEL . . . Mr. Katz has a lot of fun with dumb cops and hypocritical basketball team owners. . . . Get *Murder off the Glass*. You'll like it."
>—*The New York Times Book Review*

"AN AGREEABLE, PROMISING MYSTERY-COMEDY DEBUT—thanks to a genial sleuth-hero, an amusingly crass Watson, and a bright, breezy Chicago sports milieu. . . . Atmospheric fun."
>—*Kirkus Reviews*

MURDER OFF THE GLASS

Michael J. Katz

PUBLISHED BY POCKET BOOKS NEW YORK

This novel is a work of fiction. Names, characters, places and incidents are either the product of the author's imagination or are used fictitiously. Any resemblance to actual events or locales or persons, living or dead, is entirely coincidental.

POCKET BOOKS, a division of Simon & Schuster, Inc.
1230 Avenue of the Americas, New York, N.Y. 10020

Published by arrangement with Walker and Company
Library of Congress Catalog Card Number: 86-22463

ISBN: 0-671-64667-2

First Pocket Books printing January 1988

10 9 8 7 6 5 4 3 2 1

POCKET and colophon are trademarks of
Simon & Schuster, Inc.

Printed in the U.S.A.

1

THERE WERE FORTY-FOUR seconds left in the third quarter of a professional basketball game between the Chicago Flames and the Phoenix Suns when the lights went out. Sly Thomas, one of the Flames' guards, had just lifted a high, arching jump shot from the corner; as the small crowd hushed, waiting for the ball to complete its trajectory, the great banks of phosphorous lights flickered and went dim, the Chicago Stadium went black, and Sly Thomas's jump shot disappeared into the night.

At courtside, the confusion that followed was only slightly less than the normal chaos that accompanied the Flames, a team that had won only seventeen of fifty-five games prior to the evening's activities. "Swish!" shouted Sly Thomas to a man he assumed in the dark to be the referee, but who was actually the Phoenix trainer. "It be right in there, Murphy! Didn' touch nothin' but cord—"

"Excuse me," said the trainer, fumbling in his pocket for the small flashlight he carried to examine the battered ears and eyeballs of his players. He found the miniature light and pointed it in Thomas's direction.

"Aw, shit, man, you ain't no ref—" Sly Thomas spun around, hands on his hips, searching the darkness for a striped shirt, then groped for the trainer. "Hey wait, man, don't be leavin' with that light. . . ." The trainer had wandered back toward the Phoenix bench. "Hey wait, Doc, I got an earache. . . ."

Several yards down the floor, a few feet beside the basketball court and between the players' benches, Andy Sussman clutched his microphone, waiting for some sign of electronic life that would signal the resumption of his radio broadcast. Sussman, immersed as usual in the flow of the game, had been the last human being in the Stadium to realize what had happened. "Ronny Long brings it upcourt for the Flames," he had chanted, calling the game in his crisp cadence that made the contest seem like a forty-eight–minute horse race. "Over the time line to Branch, into the corner to Sly Thomas; Thomas has Draper all over him—don't take that shot, Sly—ten on the timer, Sly *does* shoot, a high archer, it's . . . it's . . ." An uncharacteristic silence followed, then: "It's *dark*. . . . The lights are off, ladies and gentlemen, the lights just went off here at the Stadium. Sly Thomas took a long jump shot, with Draper *all over him*—I can't see what's going on here, there's not a single light on in the entire building, all the electricity is off and . . . *fuck—I'm off!* We're off the air. Jesus Christ!"

Sussman had dropped the microphone onto the table and tapped his headphone, hoping for some instructions from his engineer, or at least some static, but he heard nothing. Oh well, he mused, catching his breath after twenty minutes of frenetic play-by-play, it was probably just as well. He had run out of adjectives trying to describe Thomas's jump shot, a top spinning, crooked-elbowed bazooka that he launched at least fifteen times a game. Occasionally, Sly's jumper would find its way through the basket, but more often—66 percent of the time, according to the up-to-date statistics that had been rushed to him at halftime—the ball would bound off the rim, or ricochet off the glass, or graze the outstretched hand of an opposing player, or sometimes just return harmlessly to earth, untouched by earthly elements since it had left Sly's hand. Andy Sussman figured that if you discounted the minuscule chance of Sly Thomas's jump shot actually falling through the net, the next best thing that could happen would be for it not to come down. It was a wonderful break for the Flames, Sussman decided, as he searched in the dark for his cup of beer.

The Stadium, by this time, had fallen into an eerie silence. The old building was located on the near West Side of Chicago, in a neighborhood Sussman cheerfully rated as one of the ten worst in the civilized world—maybe not as bad as some places he had read about in El Salvador or Calcutta, but certainly in a league with Harlem or Watts. Sussman would never drive anywhere near this place at night if there was not a basketball game going on, and he did not even like to drive by it in the daytime, when the burnt-out buildings, barren since the riots following Martin Luther King's assassination in 1968, seemed to smolder in the frigid winter air like an urbanized Mount St. Helens.

An undercurrent of fear swept through the Stadium, the meager crowd of about four thousand hoping that the electricity would return before neighborhood gangs invaded the crippled building and began sweeping through the aisles, looting the box-seat patrons, ripping off watches a row at a time, like some sort of International Harvester corn reaper. They waited for some sign of power and authority, such as the mighty organ at the east end of the building or the voice of the PA man. What they got, finally—actually, only a minute later, but it seemed like an eternity—was the little twinkle of emergency lighting, the yellow glow of two hundred "emergency exit" lamps slowly illuminating the aisles, a perfect guide for the black

7

and Latino gangs to come pillaging through the mezzanine.

"Testing, testing," said Andy Sussman, tapping his mike. "Ralph, can you boys hear me out there?" He thought he detected some static, but it was only the sound of Lester Beldon's silk shirt sliding against the torn upholstery of his customized leopard-skin card chair. Another bonus of this blackout, Sussman decided, in addition to the disappearance of Sly Thomas's jump shot, was the opportunity not to have to look at, or listen to, Lester Beldon. Beldon was Sussman's partner, the so-called "color man," whose job it was to augment Sussman's play-by-play with some occasional insight and anecdotes gleaned from his five years in the league with the original Flames, the group of rejects and low draft choices who had entered the league with the franchise twenty years ago. Sussman found Beldon's analysis insipid and his anecdotes repetitive and boring. Worse, Beldon had the annoying habit of starting his stories just as play was about to resume and running them through about two minutes of action, leaving Sussman to explain to his audience that while Beldon had been telling them about a gin-rummy game on a bus to Cincinnati in 1963, the opposing team had scored thirteen straight points, the Flames' center had fouled out, and the team was now nine points behind.

What made it all the more aggravating was the fact that Lester Beldon was a hero to the old-line power structure that owned the radio station they worked for, a symbol of the supposed good old days in Chicago sports, personified by the scrappy old Flames, who weren't any better than the current young Flames, but at least were mostly white, drank beer and whiskey instead of smoking dope, and didn't make $500,000 a year, guaranteed.

As Andy Sussman mulled over this and other inequities of life, he heard a flicker of static from his headphones, and the house lights went on. Four thousand sighs of relief rolled over the loge seats. Men checked their wives and their watches; satisfied that both were intact, they looked at the scoreboard to see if Sly Thomas's jumper had by some chance gone through the net.

"We're back," said Ralph Sanders, the engineer, to Andy Sussman through the headphones.

"We're back!" said Andy Sussman to his microphone. "We're live again from the Chicago Stadium, ladies and gentlemen, where the Flames are trailing the Phoenix Suns seventy-eight to sixty-two in the third quarter—"

"Sixty-*four*," interrupted Sly Thomas, leaning into Sussman's microphone. "That shot be fallin' in smooth as silk. You call that right, Sustman. 'Thomas shoots from the corner . . . it's *UP*, it's *GOOD*. Swisheroo!' There, fans, you be up to date now—"

"Thanks, Sly, for spending a few moments with us while we're waiting for the game to resume. . . ." Sussman signaled to Dwayne Reddick, the Flames' power forward, who led Thomas back to the bench. "To be honest with you, folks, I don't know whether Sly's shot went in or not. Lester Beldon, did you see that any better than I did?" Sussman turned aside to his partner, wondering if Beldon could possibly fill a few moments when the ball wasn't already in play. He found Lester slouching in the leopard-skin card chair, his hand cradling a beer cup. "Oh, Lester . . . ?" Sussman put his hand over his microphone, covering it almost, but not quite, so that the studious listener could barely hear him say, "Lester, you're not supposed to fall asleep until after the game starts."

Sussman jabbed Beldon in the shoulder, then took his hands off the mike and resumed his commentary while he tried to awaken Beldon. "Lester just got back from talking to Coach White of the Suns. What did the coach have to allow, Lester?" Sussman shook Beldon's obnoxious pink

Hawaiian shirt which he wore loose over his slacks, then slapped Beldon on the jowl. His hand came back moist and red. "Lester?" Sussman stared at Lester Beldon, as the referee blew his whistle, signaling the teams back onto the floor. "Lester?"

"Ladies and gentlemen, there are forty-four seconds left in the third quarter," the PA announcer intoned. "The score is Phoenix seventy-eight, the Flames sixty-two. . . ."

Andy Sussman wiped his bloody right hand off on the scoresheet and felt Lester Beldon's empty pulse. "Lester? Jesus Christ," Sussman said to half a million listeners in greater Chicagoland and several thousand others scattered in Iowa, Indiana, and Wisconsin. "Jesus Christ, Lester, you're dead!"

2

"Was it the 'Jesus Christ,' Mr. Brandt? That's all I want to know, if I'm being suspended for invoking the name of your Savior after the person sitting next to me turns out to have a bullet in his back—"

"Now, Andy, let's try to be professional about all this. There were several mitigating factors behind the decision. . . ."

Andy Sussman loosened his tie and sunk into the chair that sat across from the desk of Wilfred P. Brandt, the general manager of WCGO radio. Sussman was wearing a dark blue suit, a white shirt, and a solid blue tie—a uniform specifically tailored for meetings with Brandt or other WCGO executives. Sussman, to his memory, had worn the suit exactly five times—at his original interview, when he was officially hired two weeks later, and at the three year-end conferences when he had received contract extensions and pay raises. Sussman had attempted several times to deduct the suit as a business expense, a request that was disallowed, unfairly he thought, by the IRS.

Wilfred P. Brandt, also dressed in a blue suit and a white shirt, sat stiffly in his plush leather desk chair. He was in his mid-fifties, with closely cropped hair slicked down by hair cream and a slight pudge that perspired through his white shirt at the navel. He was typical in most ways of the WCGO career executive; that is to say, his entire wardrobe, lifestyle, and world view could be summed up in a few pages of the 1957 Sears catalog.

"Mr. Brandt," Sussman implored, "I'd like to resolve this situation as amicably as possible, but I'm going to have to insist on a more specific reason for a suspension without pay—"

"Harummmph," said Wilfred P. Brandt. "Mr. Sussman, we do have a murder situation here, involving a man you were closely associated with. I wouldn't think much more elaboration would be necessary."

"Mr. Brandt, there must be fifty people at this station who worked with Les Beldon at one time or another. Surely you can't be implying that I'm a suspect in this case—"

"Excuse me, Mr. Sussman." Brandt reached for his telephone, a multi-buttoned touch-tone receiver that had only recently replaced his all-black, pre-Sputnik model. "Miss Rand, could you send in Detective Lafferty, please?" He then waited stiffly, as if further conversation might brand him an accessory to the crime.

Detective Lafferty entered, a tall, angular man with a slight stoop, whose dark-blue trench coat was buttoned halfway to the top. He walked past the remaining leather chair, opting for a more spartan chrome model. He acknowledged Sussman's presence with a nod, let out a tubercular cough, and began reviewing the facts of the case in a phlegm-spattered mumble. "The victim, one Lester Beldon, employed by radio station WCGO as a basketball analyst . . . cause of death: bullet wound through the back and chest . . . small firearm with silencer . . . time of death: approximately nine-twenty-five, Tuesday evening, February fifteenth . . ." He recited several more statistics, including the caliber of the bullet and the probable length of distance on impact, which he estimated to be three feet.

Then he turned to Sussman. "Now Mr. Sussman, it's common knowledge that you and Mr. Beldon were not the best of friends—"

"We had some professional differences, Detective Lafferty—"

Lafferty wheezed again and pulled out a yellowed copy of the *Arlington Heights Bulletin,* dated December 17, 1981. ". . . totally lacking in even the most rudimentary knowledge of basketball . . . speaks English as a second language . . . typical of the sentimental old fatheads that have been languishing at WCGO for the past decade . . ."

Sussman drew his lips. The interview had been a mistake—he had figured the paper for a suburban throwaway, not realizing how the western suburbs had burgeoned while he was out in the sticks, building his résumé at small stations in Bozeman and Reno and Green Bay. The story had ended up being quoted in the *Trib* and the *Sun-Times,* and although Sussman's popularity had immediately skyrocketed with the city's true basketball fans, he had become a black sheep at the offices of WCGO, his employment continuing only through the insistence of the Flames' management. "Granted," Sussman shrugged, "we were not the best of friends . . ."

"Lester Beldon was one of the most beloved sportscasters in the WCGO family," said Wilfred P. Brandt, sounding like he was testing the eulogy he was scheduled to give that afternoon. "He had hundreds of thousands of fans in greater Chicagoland. He was one of the original Flames, Andy, as I'm sure you know. Why, just the mail he received was greater than our entire staff of on-the-air personnel put together. . . ."

"I know, Mr. Brandt." Andy Sussman wished he could have shared some of that mail with Brandt; most of it was along the lines of "Please fire that senile old asshole." Sussman knew—he had rummaged through Beldon's wastebasket several times during his infrequent forays into the office.

"Mr. Sussman," coughed Detective Lafferty, "we simply had to make a list of anyone who might have had reason to wish ill will upon the victim—"

"Detective, you're not actually suggesting that *I* murdered Les Beldon—"

"A preliminary list, Mr. Sussman. Could have done it. Had reason to do it."

"You're suggesting that I somehow arranged for the Stadium power to black out, then pulled a gun out of my pocket, shot Lester Beldon in the back, and made the gun vanish into thin air?"

"Mr. Sussman, all of our evidence has to be considered shaky at the moment. We simply had to let your superiors know of the direction our investigation is taking."

Wilfred Brandt walked over to Sussman and placed a corporate palm on his shoulder. "Try to consider the image of WCGO, Andy. I just think it would be best for the station, considering your rather ill-disguised disdain for Lester, if we had a brief cooling-off period until the police are able to find some leads, or at least find a motive that would clear you of any wrongdoing."

Sussman knew that he should have brought a lawyer with him. Even in his simplest disputes with station management, such as over obtaining a company parking sticker, he had found it impossible to make any progress without being able to substantiate that his civil rights were being violated. "Mr. Brandt," he said, "I think I can state with the most complete confidence that suspending me without pay, on suspicion of a crime there's not a shred of evidence to suggest I committed, is an action that won't be accepted by any court in this country. Furthermore, in regard to compensatory damages regarding my injured reputation—"

"Of course, Andy," interrupted Wilfred P. Brandt, "there *are* other factors. We do have to consider the 'Jesus Christ.' "

Sussman sank a few inches further into the chair.

"I think we've made our on-the-air standards rather clear on this point, Andy. And I further believe we've issued several documented warnings to you regarding your use of profanity directly previous and subsequent to live broadcasts. The listeners of WCGO do not, Andy, consider the expression 'Jesus Christ' an appropriate way to exhibit surprise, or excitement, or even—as this case may have been—profound dismay."

"Jesus Christ," muttered Sussman, immediately thinking of several ways in which his use of those words could be construed as an affirmation of religious commitment, clearly under the protection of the First Amendment. He could maintain that in the brief moments of blackout he had seen a vision of the Lord and, in a flash of sanctimony, been born again. "Jesus Christ!" he had excitedly shouted to the unfortunately dead Lester Beldon. Or perhaps, in the panic of seeing Lester's life draining away, he had taken, out of pure friendship, the responsibility of administering to his partner the final rites: "Jesus Christ . . ."

"Excuse me?" said Wilfred P. Brandt, speaking now with the power, authority and fifty thousand watts of WCGO.

"Mr. Brandt," said Andy Sussman, "I want you to know that I share your grief in the untimely death of Lester Beldon and regret any offense that might have been taken over the purely accidental use of the name of a person many of our listeners believe to be the Son of God." Sussman immediately wished he had not said that, but could not resist the look of extreme nausea it brought to Brandt's face. "However, I must let you know that I find your suspension to have no legal or ethical grounds, and I'll be making every possible effort to have it rescinded."

"I'm sorry you feel that way, Andy. You know, despite everything, we like to consider that you're part of the family here at WCGO."

Sussman smiled weakly. "I appreciate that, Mr. Brandt. I'm sure we'll have this straightened out in no time." Andy Sussman pulled himself out of the chair. He adjusted his tie, shook Wilfred P. Brandt's hand, and walked stiffly out of the office.

3

THE THOUGHT OF hiring a private detective—the thought that private detectives even existed in the real world—had never occurred to Andy Sussman before. Fictional characters like Charlie Chan and Sam Spade seemed far removed from Chicago's North Shore suburbs, or even his more recent surroundings in Lincoln Park. Sussman was aware that some of his friends who did business in the seedier sections of the city occasionally had need of a detective to track down a firebug or a shoplifter, but these people were not private detectives in the classic silver-screen mode. They were mostly retired cops or laid-off security men, trying to pick up a few bucks on the side. Now, though, he needed one.

The search for a private detective had been additionally challenging in that it caused Sussman to consider sidestepping his usual network for securing professional services. That network consisted principally of people with whom he had once gone to high school, summer camp, or religious school. Sussman had not planned it that way; it was only recently that he recognized that everyone whose services he now retained in a professional capacity could be found staring at him in his Bar Mitzvah pictures.

As it happened, the only Jew Sussman knew of who could be considered a choice for this mission was not a guest at his Bar Mitzvah. He was an emigré from Grosse Pointe, Michigan, whose only saving graces were that he had gone to college with Sussman at Wisconsin ten years ago and now owned two season tickets for the Flames, which he used occasionally, when the Flames won more than one game in a row. His name was Murray Glick.

Murray Glick had received his graduate degree in criminology and gone to work as a consultant for a private corporation in Chicago. He had grown restless after a few months, however, and quit to establish his own practice in Highwood, a small suburb just north of Highland Park. It had seemed, at the time, the perfect place for a Jewish private eye to set up shop; just across the border from the largest affluent Jewish population in Chicagoland, yet sufficiently shady to house an agency for private investigation. The locale had served Glick adequately for three years until, in a flash of inspiration, he decided to open up a branch office a few miles away in the glamorous Northbrook Court Shopping Mall.

"I really think it's time to get out of the hard-core, elbow-grease type cases, you know?" Murray had explained, over chocolate crêpes in the Magic Pan restaurant down the corridor from his new office. "Somebody actually shot at me the other day, can you believe it, Hoops?" He had pulled a small piece of molten lead out of the pocket of his Jordache blue denim jacket and showed it to Sussman. "Alienation of affection, for Chrissakes. And she wasn't even that good looking. For that I get a bullet up my ass?" He put the slug away. "I just figure, Hoopsie, look at the clientele here: you've got your Highland Park and Glencoe population; you've got your Neiman-Marcus, your Lord and Taylor—it's a natural, if I can just tailor my business to the location."

And so Glick had opened up his branch of Glick Investigations in a small storefront in Northbrook Court, directly between Fannie May Candies and the Foot Locker athletic-shoe store. He had originally taken on a partner, but Sussman guessed that today, in the midst of the mall's Presidents' Day sale, Murray would be running the operation himself.

"Hoops!" said Murray Glick, peeking from behind a *People* magazine. "You're a fright, man." He extended a hairy hand toward Sussman, exchanged a firm handshake, then straightened out the wrinkles in Sussman's sweater. "You sleep in that thing, Andrew? There's a sale over at Justin's, you know. Cashmere sweaters, twenty percent off, velour shirts half price, this weekend only. Presidents' Day, one of my favorite holidays . . ."

Sussman walked past the imaginary threshold that marked the entrance to Glick Investigations and looked at the small posters in front of the empty secretary's desk:

ASK ABOUT OUR SPECIAL PRESIDENTS' DAY RATES.
THIS WEEKEND ONLY, 10–30% OFF.
GIFTS, SECRETS. PLEASE RING FOR SERVICE.

Sussman rang.

"I heard about poor Les Beldon," Glick said, taking a bite from a Slice-O-Pizza that had been resting on a paper plate. "Poor dumb fuck. I'm telling you, Hoops, you gotta stay away from neighborhoods like that. I only go when they win two or three in a row, you know? That's when they get crowds. They assign police to the place, not just a couple of cops sitting at the door—"

"Murray," said Sussmann, reaching for a half-opened bag of potato chips, "I got suspended today."

Murray Glick put the *People* magazine down. "Suspended? Geez, Hoops, how'd you do that? You didn't sing that Australian drinking song I taught you on the air again—"

"I'm a suspect in the murder of Lester Beldon, Murray." There followed a long silence, by which Glick was apparently making clear that "murder" was not a welcome word in the Northbrook Court branch of Glick Investigations. "I'm not what you would call a 'solid' suspect," Sussman continued. "Actually, there's not one iota of evidence to suggest I had anything to do with it, which of course I didn't. Unfortunately, the expletive I uttered at the sight of the recently departed's corpse—"

"Yeah, yeah," Glick said. "So you pushed the boys at 'CGO a little too far this time, right?"

"I didn't push them at all, Murray. What was I supposed to say?"

Glick put his pizza back on the plate and washed it down with an Orange Julius.

"Murray, they're going to drag this investigation on for months. They have no idea who murdered Lester Beldon or why. They have nothing to go on, they have no—"

A hand reached in front of Sussman and rang the bell on Glick's desk. The hand belonged to a middle-aged woman who had dyed-black hair and was wearing a beige-and-green pants suit.

"Excuse me," said Glick. "Can I help you, ma'am?"

"Are you Mr. Glick?"

"That's right."

"I'm Mrs. Brenner, I called you this morning."

"Ah yes, Mrs. Brenner. Why don't we go back to my office . . . ?"

Mrs. Brenner emitted a slightly nervous laugh and sat down in the chair next to Sussman. "Well, that all sounds so hush-hush, Mr. Glick, and I don't think it's really necessary. You see, the problem is . . ." She took a passport from her purse and opened it, to reveal the picture of Mr. Edward Morton Brenner. "I'm so embarrassed, it's the only picture I've got of him that's not framed somewhere. Can you take a copy of it or something?''

"We've got a copy machine in the back, Mrs. Brenner.''

"It's Ed's birthday in two weeks, Mr. Glick. It's his fiftieth. That's such a big one, you know, and I just never know what to get him. He has everything he needs after all, and when he wants something—well, he just goes out and *gets* it, you know what I mean?''

"I see," said Glick, lighting up a cigar. "And I don't suppose you've thought of asking him?''

"I do, I ask him all the time! He says, 'Surprise me,' and then I surprise him with something, and he gives me this look like I just bought him something radioactive—''

"Mrs. Brenner—''

"Here," said Mrs. Brenner, pulling a list of names and addresses out of her purse. "He belongs to Northmoor Country Club. He plays bridge there, even in the winter. He takes steams at the Standard Club every day at noon. I bet he talks to the guys there all the time. I'm sure if you just get in a bridge game with him or something . . .''

"Hmm . . .'' Glick opened his secretary's desk drawer and pulled out a contract form. "You understand, Mrs. Brenner, I work on an hourly rate, plus expenses. . . .''

Mrs. Brenner tittered. "Oh yes . . . well, actually, this *is* the first time I've hired a detective. And I did see your sign about the Presidents' Day Sale.''

"Right, it's a good thing you stopped in today. Ah, Peggy?''

Glick's secretary returned from her coffee break with a Diet 7-Up and a gyros sandwich.

"Peggy, could you run Mrs. Brenner through the formal contract here, then buzz me in my office?''

"Sure, Mr. Glick.''

"Oh, I'm sorry if I interrupted," Mrs. Brenner said. "Actually, I didn't realize you were who you were. . . ."

"No problem, Mrs. Brenner. I'll go through all the paperwork tonight, and I'll be in touch with you twice a week." Glick grabbed Sussman and led him toward the back office. "It was nice to meet you, Mrs. Brenner."

"Oh, it was my pleasure."

Glick closed the door behind him and settled his six-foot frame into a brown leather desk chair. "Wonderful lady, isn't she, Hoopsie?" he said, relighting his cigar.

"Murray, I'm beginning to worry about you."

Murray Glick puffed a ring of cigar smoke and let it drift aimlessly through his office. "Business is good, Hoops. Just this month alone, I'm running through nine or ten cases."

"Finding out what Uncle Charlie wants for Christmas?"

"And what dress Mrs. Jefferson's wearing to the Crystal Ball. And what Bob Graber's real golf handicap is. And whether that cute little cheerleader at Highland Park High has herpes."

"God, you're a slime, Murray."

"Oh yeah? You think that kid over at the sporting goods store wouldn't trade a few weeks' pay to find out? You think I'm not providing a public service besides?"

"Murray—"

"The point is, Hoops, it's a whole new ballgame. It's exceeded my expectations. I don't need to put myself at risk anymore. I may even close Highwood and open up another branch at Old Orchard, or maybe Water Tower Place. Care for a cigar?"

Sussman reached for one of Glick's Don Diegos and pulled the wrapper off slowly, cutting the end off with Glick's cigar trimmer and tapping it softly on Glick's leather-covered desk. "Murray," he said, "I come to you in a moment of need. I have a potentially rewarding career in the field of sports journalism, which is being put in jeopardy by the actions of my employers. I've had network offers, did you know that, Murray?''

Glick tapped some ashes out of his cigar.

"College football scoreboard, halftime highlights, that sort of thing. Nothing I'd take right now, of course, but if a play-by-play spot opens up—''

"It sounds very promising, Hoops. Maybe you should tell 'CGO to stuff it, so to speak.''

"Murray, every day they hold me under suspicion of this murder, my career goes irrevocably deeper into the sewer. Do you understand that? No network is going to touch me, no other station in Chicago is going to make me an offer—''

"You could have one hell of a lawsuit, Andrew. I'd call Susie right away if I were you. She could fix you up for life. She might even go out with you, if she got you a big enough settlement.''

"I've considered that, Murray.''

"Dating Susie?''

Sussman grabbed Glick's gold cigar lighter and lit up his cigar. "Murray, do we need to go over our high-school civics again? WCGO has resources in this city whose clout extends far beyond a date with Susie Ettenger. They have a television station. They have a PR firm. They also have a legal position, albeit a slim one, to keep me under suspension until this thing gets resolved, which could take one hell of a long time.''

Murray Glick rolled his cigar in his mouth, taking short, staccato puffs.

"Murray . . . ,'' said Sussman. "Murray, you owe me.''

"I *owe* you?''

"Hell, yes. For Sly Thomas, in case you forgot.''

"Oh, yeah."

"Don't give me 'oh yeah.' I bet his fee paid for all this glitzy furniture in here. Plush leather desk. Don Diego cigars. When'd you stop smoking White Owls, Murray?"

Glick smiled, balancing the cigar in the corner of his mouth. "I will admit that an occasional client whose predicament and annual salary allows me to collect a fee in excess of normal circumstances is always appreciated."

"I should hope so." Good old Sly, Sussman thought. During his rookie season, Thomas had rented a condominium a few blocks from Northbrook Court. One day he had wandered into the mall and tried to pick up a girl who was working in the stereo department of Sears; the result had been a charge of statutory rape by the girl's father. Sussman had referred Thomas to Murray, who had proven that their activities together consisted wholly of a shared taco-dog and a pineapple milk shake. Glick had also been able to show that during the nights in question, the girl had been occupied with fellow workers in the stereo department, as well as several members of the sports department and the garden department. The father had quietly dropped the complaint.

"All right, Hoops," said Glick, "let's go over a few things theoretically, working on the assumption that I might take this case, if there is a case at all. We start with the lights going out, and we end up with Les Beldon being shot to death, right?"

"That's a beginning, Murray."

"Now, you'll want to go down to the Stadium, talk to the engineers down there, find out what caused the blackout—"

"Me?"

"Then you'll want to retrace everything Lester Beldon did on the last day of his life, and for that matter review

24

everything he did over the last couple of months, see who his enemies were, if he had any besides you—"

"I'm supposed to do this? Murray, I'm trying to hire *you*."

Murray Glick snuffed his cigar out. "Hoops, listen. I run a nice, quiet little agency here, okay? Even in Highwood, I don't do murders. You think your wife's cheating on you, you think your partner's siphoning off the profits, you give me a call. And even that, Hoops, even that I stay away from now. Mrs. Brenner, Mr. Graber, that's my clientele. Murders I don't touch." He sank back in his chair and fondled a paperweight, inside of which he had implanted the lead slug that had been fired at him several months before. "A relic, Andrew. And a reminder. Murderers are dangerous. They kill people."

Sussman pondered his cigar. "And all this hypothetical analysis you're going through?"

"Andrew, I offer you, free of charge, all the analytical skills which I have accumulated through four years of college in criminology, two years in graduate school, and five years in the business. I'll evaluate every piece of evidence you find, listen to every story, watch every videotape. Just do the legwork and bring everything in to me, right here at the mall." He extended his right arm. "A deal, Hoopsie?"

"You're a big help, Murray."

"Hey, don't knock it, I charge a hundred dollars a day for that. Besides, you really don't want me snooping around down there, do you? The cops won't like it if they see me around, especially before they even have a chance to get started. Just do your homework and bring it in to me, all right?"

Sussman and Glick shook hands.

"And call Susie Ettenger, Hoops. Sue those bastards, that's the only way you'll get through to 'em." Glick led

Sussman out of his office, back outside where his secretary was arranging Mrs. Brenner's papers into a file. "You ought to check the sales around here before you go, Andrew. Midwest Stereo's got a price on tape decks, Florsheim's got some real nice suede shoes . . ."

"I'll check it out," said Sussman, wandering back into the mainstream of the mall.

"Do your homework," shouted Murray Glick. "I'll talk to you soon. Happy Presidents' Day!"

4

"THERE'S FIVE SECONDS left in the game, fans, as the Flames bring the ball downcourt. *Three . . . two . . .* Holmes looks for a shot. *One.* Time has *run out.* That's right, fans, time has run out, and so have I—but I'll be back in just a few minutes, so if you'll leave your name and number when you hear the beep, I'll return your call as soon as I get back."

The beep sounded, followed by a voice identifying itself in a somber tone as Channel 7 News. It left a number, then hung up, leaving a dial tone humming into the message machine.

Andy Sussman noted the flashing message light and ignored it. He stretched himself out on his couch, kicked off his shoes, and turned up the television volume by remote control. He had been switching channels on the six o'clock news, all four of which had been carrying highlights of Lester Beldon's funeral. "Lester Beldon was one of the most beloved sportscasters in the WCGO family," Wilfred Brandt was saying in eulogy. "He was one of the original Flames, as we all know, and he had hundreds of thousands of fans in the greater Chicago area—"

Sussman switched to Channel 7, which apparently had managed to piece together a broadcast without any contributions from him. They were showing highlights of Les-

27

ter's career—faded pictures of his high school basketball team at Lane Tech, film highlights of his college days at Michigan State, eroding videotapes of his days with the Flames. The videotapes carried a small trailer at the bottom of the screen which read: "Courtesy of WCGO-TV."

The telephone rang again. This time, after the recording, a voice said: "Andy Sussman, you're being very rude. You're either in some bar getting drunk, or you're sitting there screening calls. You were supposed to call me about Saturday night, remember? I've got two tickets to the symphony. . . ." There was a slight pause. "All right, Andy, I'm just going to stay on the line a few seconds. I'll give you a chance to pick up the phone. . . ." Sussman turned the TV volume off and sat rigidly quiet. He did not think the machine could transmit sound while the phone was on the hook, but it was best not to take chances. He remained perfectly still for about ten seconds, until the voice said, "Oh, fuck you, Andy," and hung up.

Sussman was pleased that he had evoked an obscenity from the lips of Wendy Altman. She was altogether too uptight, and Sussman felt that a little overt rage and frustration would be a positive thing for their relationship. Perhaps she would progress from swearing into his answering machine to a shrieking, "Fuck you, Andy!" in the middle of the Civic Opera House. It was almost worth calling her back. On the other hand, Wendy, as usual, seemed completely oblivious to his personal situation. He could understand how she might be a little slow in learning about Lester Beldon's death, since she never listened to his broadcasts or read the sports pages. By now, however, the news was all over the city, and it took a pretty concentrated show of indifference for her to ignore the situation completely. She was symptomatic, Sussman thought, of Category A of the girls he dated: women recommended by his mother. Girls in that group tended to view him as a well-educated, self-supporting man of good breeding who had temporarily involved himself in a job which had something to do with sports and required him to be in smelly gymnasiums on Friday and Saturday nights. They were distinguishable from girls in Group B, who were usually rabid basketball fans, or at least regular attenders of basketball games. These girls hung around Sussman's broadcast table before and after games, followed him down to the locker room, tailed him to bars and restaurants. Sussman preferred not to think of these girls as groupies—they exhibited such a noble dedication to the game and its odd and sometimes exhausting rituals. A little attention to them once in a while had not seemed such a terrible thing.

Then, of course, there was Category C. Category C girls were warm and understanding, but with a good sense of occasional raunchiness. They were able to appreciate the athletic grace of professional basketball and the journalistic talent it took to describe it night after night. Category C girls were self-sufficient; they could handle real world jobs like law or medicine, although they would gladly give them up, at least temporarily, to raise a family with the right man. Sussman had never actually dated a Category C girl; the only one he knew was Susie Ettenger, and she would not go near him, except on business.

Sussman turned the volume back up on the TV and switched to Channel 2, which was showing a tape of the final seconds prior to the fatal blackout. All the Flames home games were shown on subscription television; the local stations picked up the highlights for their sports segments, erasing the soundtrack and inserting simulated crowd reactions at key spots. Sussman listened and watched as Sly Thomas went up for his jump shot, accompanied by a swell of excitement from the phony crowd.

Sussman's phone rang again, and he listened to his tape recording for the fourteenth time. He would have to think up a new message, he decided, just to let people know he was still alive.

"Hello, Andy?" said a voice. "It's Susan . . . Ettenger. I got your message—I guess you already know that—"

"Hello?" said Sussman, picking up the receiver. "Susie?"

"Well, this is certainly an honor. Do you always talk to people after the fifth message, or was it just a random choice?"

"I just walked in," Sussman lied. He turned the television down. "I was watching the news. . . ."

"Poor Lester Beldon's funeral highlights?"

"I was hoping to get Brandt's eulogy on the Betamax."

Susie Ettenger sighed. "Andy Sussman, what are we going to do with you?"

Sussman smiled, for the first time that day. Did he detect some personal concern here, or was it just professional responsibility?

"Let me ask you before we go any further, just for my clarification," Susie said. "Did you do it?"

"Did I *what?*" Sussman's spirits plunged twenty-seven stories, down to the underground parking lot of his Lincoln Park high-rise.

"Well, you know, I mean, I don't believe you'd do anything like that personally, but just for the record . . ."

"Miss Ettenger, as God be my witness, I had nothing to do with the death of Lester Beldon."

"Okay," said Susie, not too convincingly. "I'll accept that. And you have no idea who did do it, or who might have had any reason to do it?"

"Susie, unless I missed something on one of my messages, I haven't been indicted for anything. I'm just trying to get my good name and my job back."

"Right."

Sussman heard the rustle of papers next to the telephone. "Are you still at the office?"

"Of course I'm still at the office."

Sorry I asked, thought Sussman. He had meant to suggest that they discuss the situation over dinner, but he put the idea aside.

"You realize, Andy, that your constant antagonization of the management at WCGO is coming back to haunt you."

"I'm not asking them to kiss and make up, Susie. I just want my rights protected. Hell, threaten 'em with a lawsuit—violation of contract, damage to reputation. I'm sure their grudge doesn't extend all the way to the back of their bank account."

"It's going to take a hell of a lot more time and money than you've got, Andy, to get to the back of WCGO's bank account."

Sussman flicked the television to WCGO-TV, which had finished its special report on Lester Beldon's death and was now showing "Family Feud." "Are you telling me you can't even get a simple injunction against them, Susie? Believe me, the last thing Wilfred Brandt wants to do is get hauled into court. . . ."

"Andy!"

She's exasperated, Sussman thought. It's almost 6:30. She's got places to go, probably some international banker taking her out for dinner . . .

"Andy, all I'm saying is that we're much better off maintaining an amicable relationship with WCGO. I'm sure we can help them realize that they aren't improving their image any by placing one of their most visible employees under suspicion of murder, and that's what it amounts to, whatever their reasons for suspending you. What was it you said this time?"

"Jesus Christ."

" 'Jesus Christ'?"

Sussman thought he detected a snicker on the other end of the line.

"Terrific, Andy. Only a Jew could get suspended for saying 'Jesus Christ' on the radio."

"Cute, Suse. I'll tell you what. Why don't we meet for lunch tomorrow. We can talk things over, then head over to 'CGO and straighten things out. I promise I'll behave."

"Lunch? I don't think so, Andy, I've got meetings all morning, I probably won't be free till two o'clock. Why don't I make an appointment with Wilfred Brandt for two-thirty? I'll meet you over there."

"Fine."

"Oh, and Andy?"

"What?"

"Can I take you up on that?"

"On what? For lunch sometime?"

"To behave."

"Oh. Yeah, I'll do my best."

"Good. Don't worry, Andy, you'll be back on the air in no time. So long now."

"Bye-bye, Susie," said Andy Sussman to the dead telephone line. "Bye-bye, love," he added, humming now to his remote control. "Bye-bye, happiness . . ." He rolled off the couch and headed for the refrigerator, where he pulled out half of a ham sandwich, left over from last month's Super Bowl party. "Hello, loneliness, I think I'm gonna—" He eyed the sandwich, then pulled out a beer. Cry? Die? He flicked the TV set back on. "Hmm," he said. He popped the top off his beer. He grabbed a box of Wheat Thins, yawned and settled back to watch "Family Feud."

5

ANDY SUSSMAN PULLED into the Stadium parking lot the next morning, noting that his parking space was still reserved, an oversight he assumed would be corrected as soon as WCGO got around to assigning someone else to do the next broadcast. He was dressed in his blue suit for his afternoon meeting with Wilfred Brandt; he loosened his tie as he crossed the empty floor and headed for the dank, steamy Stadium locker room, where the Flames players were lounging after a morning shoot-around.

"Hey, Sustman!" shouted Sly Thomas, his naked body half-covered by the whirlpool suds. "Where you be yesterday, man? We all lookin' for you at Lester's funeral. We thought you be a pall bearer for sure, man, throw ol' Lester right in the hole yourself."

"Yeah, well," Sussman said, surveying the collection of mostly black bodies, looking for the muscular torso and flecked goatee of Dwayne Reddick. "I was just so torn with grief, Sly, I didn't want to break down and cry in front of everybody—"

"You be torn with grief, my ass. You prob'ly over at Faces, celebratin' with them horny white chicks always hangin' round your table. Who they gonna give you for a partner now, anyway? They give you your choice, this time, Sustman?"

"Sly, I've got some bad news for you—"

"Maybe you pick a brother this time. Get some real analysis, steada that 1960s Greyhound Bus rides fairy-tale shit. Maybe I retire, join you in the booth." Sly grabbed a can of diet soda from the side of the whirlpool and held it up to his mouth like a microphone. "Sly Thomas here, sports fans, tellin' you what be comin' *down* with this basketball team—"

"Sly, I don't know how to break this to you, but I think you're going to have to find someone else to apologize to for your jump shots the next few games."

"What's that, man?"

"I've been suspended. Just for a game or two, hopefully, until they straighten out the mess with Lester Beldon."

"Suspended?" Sly Thomas rose from the whirlpool, naked except for an Ace bandage around his left elbow. "Suspended? Man, how they do that? I thought they's one big happy fam'ly over there at 'CGO. You be a regular part of the schedule, like Dick Van Dyke or Mary Tyler Moore. They can't suspend you."

Sussman backed away from the whirlpool, not anxious to get chlorinated soap suds all over his suit.

"Whatta they think, Sustman, they think you did it? They think you greased fat old Lester Beldon?"

"Hard to say, Sly. Look, is Dwayne around?"

"I don't know, I'll check." Sly shook some suds out of his ears. "Whoa, brother Andrew takin' the rap." He cupped his hands and shouted at the top of his voice. "Hey, Reddick!" His voice was drowned out by the whirlpool, which had just been turned on again. "Oh, Du-aane!" He turned to a smallish, wiry Latino who was crawling into the water. "Hey, Flame, what you doin' in there?"

"Gotta soak for thirty minutes twice a day," said the

man. "For the knee, doctor's orders. Hey, Andy, how's it hangin'?"

"It's hanging fine, Señor," said Sussman. "What brings you to the SS Thomas this morning?"

"Cartilage in the knee, man. I think I'm out for the rest of the homestand. They may do an arthroscopy next week if it doesn't get better."

"Geez, what a team." Sussman shook his head. The man in the whirlpool was Señor Flame, the team mascot, and it was altogether typical of the Flames' fortunes that even their mascot had ended up on the disabled list. The knee injury would be especially crippling for the Señor, whose real name Sussman had never learned. Señor Flame's contributions to the team consisted of snakelike voodoo dances which he performed in the aisles during time-outs, dressed in a mangy orange-and-blue flame costume which covered his face and rose to a tapered tip three feet over his head, making him look like an overgrown pilot light. Although Señor Flame had begun his act on his own, dancing through the box seats to the Stadium organist's rendition of "Great Balls of Fire," he had become so popular that the Flames had made him a paid employee this season. There was no telling what the knee injury would do to his career, Sussman thought, although at least he was on the Flames' medical plan now and could receive proper treatment.

"Reddick!" Sly Thomas shouted, raising his voice above the whirlpool. *"Du-aane!"*

A tall, sturdy black man, dressed in black slacks and leather boots but bare from the waist up, ambled over to the whirlpool. "Dwayne," he said to Sly Thomas, in a deep, gravelly voice, stressing the single syllable. "Not 'Du-ane.' Dwayne."

"Hey, right, bro. Du-ane." Sly smiled a nervous, gap-tooth smile and descended back into the whirlpool.

Reddick glared at Thomas, then patted Sussman on the back. "How ya doin', Andy?"

"All right, considering the circumstances."

"Yeah, man, I heard." Reddick pulled a T-shirt over his chest and tucked it into his slacks. "Amazing business you're in there. C'mon over to Doctor D's office before I get all sweaty again, we'll see what we can do for you." He grabbed Sussman by the arm and directed him toward the back of the locker room.

"Hey, Sustman, man, don't you worry," Sly Thomas shouted from the whirlpool. "I be on your side, I be backin' you up all the way."

"Yeah, all the way to Joliet," said Dwayne Reddick, leading Sussman through the maze of lockers. Reddick was in his third year with the Flames, a former all-American center from Michigan and one of the few Flames players who had actually earned a degree. He had, in fact, been accepted to law school at Ann Arbor, but had delayed entrance in favor of a five-year, 1.4-million-dollar no-cut contract in Chicago.

Reddick's reputation on the Flames was that of the consummate professional. He had made the transition from college center to professional power forward with little difficulty, making the all-star team his last two years. He was always physically fit and mentally prepared, not only for each game but for the particular opponent he would be matched up against. He kept a video cassette recorder in his locker area, along with a collection of videotapes of every game the Flames played, so he could evaluate his performance and pick out flaws in his opponents' games. It was the tapes that Sussman hoped might provide some insight into the events of two days ago.

"Hey, I really feel bad about this, Andy," Reddick said, loading a tape into his unit. "I wish I could remember what was going on out there. You get so caught up in the game, though . . ."

"It was all pretty confusing, once the lights went out. I was hoping maybe the tapes might show something."

"Of course, if my prelaw courses mean anything, I don't think they can hold you back for too long. What was it you said again?"

"Jesus Christ."

Reddick laughed. "Oh happy day," he sang, in his deep, rumbling baritone. "Oh, happy day . . . when Jeeesus walked—"

"Hey, keep it down over there!" shouted a voice.

"Excuse me, brothers?" Reddick poked his goatee over the top of the lockers, into the adjoining cubicle.

"We're meditating," said the voice, which belonged to Jack Bryce, the starting center. "Relaxation therapy, man. Fifteen minutes is like six hours' sleep. You should try it, Dwayne, it'll get you ready for games, 'specially on the road. Works better'n greenies."

"Yeah, terrific," Reddick muttered. He turned the video recorder on, keeping the volume low. "Okay," he said to Sussman, "you saw the blackout part, I take it?"

"At least fifty times."

Reddick wound the tape back, projecting a collage of backward-jumping players and reverse jump shots onto the screen. "There. Two minutes before the lights went out, we'll play it right to the end."

"Gotcha," said Sussman, peering into the corners of the screen. The fixed camera positions at the Stadium, he knew, were situated just below the balcony, above and behind his courtside broadcasting position. That meant that the view of him and Lester Beldon, if there was one, was of the backs of their heads. The only times they ever appeared on camera was if one of the two floor cameras picked up some action right in front of them, such as an argument with an official or a scramble for the ball.

Sussman hunched forward, squinting at the screen as Reddick ran the crucial two minutes back and forth. "Dwayne, you got the second quarter on here?"

"Yeah."

"Run it back, halfway. I think there was a bad pass in there somewhere, ended up in Lester's lap."

Reddick ran the tape back slowly.

"There."

Reddick stopped the tape. A Flames player had thrown the ball out of bounds, near midcourt. The director had cut to the floor camera, which showed a blustering Lester Beldon, holding the ball next to his extra large waistline.

"Man, look at old fat Lester," Reddick said. "The man does *not* look like he expects to die before the end of the third quarter."

Sussman gave the picture a close examination. On television, Beldon's already corpulent figure was exaggerated. His six-foot–five-inch frame looked smaller, stuffed into the leopard-skin card chair, and his face looked bloated. He was wearing a pair of tan slacks, almost bursting at the crotch, and a pinkish red Hawaiian shirt which hung loosely over the belt. A plaid sport jacket could be seen draped over the chair, with a long, fur-lined overcoat slung sloppily over the sport jacket. Beldon was halfway out of his chair, his face registering a look of bewilderment as the ball bounded into his hands.

Sussman advanced the tape slowly. The camera zoomed out as Beldon returned the ball with a 1950s push pass, then the picture cut back to the fixed cameras in the balcony. Sussman ran back the tape a few seconds, then froze it. The camera had pulled back far enough so that he could see a few of the people who were sitting behind Lester Beldon. "Recognize anyone?" Sussman asked.

"Just faces to me, Andy. I try not to get too familiar with any of the regulars out there—a lot of them are bettors."

"Isn't that Charlie Hathaway?"

Reddick shrugged.

"You know, Hathaway's Pub on Dearborn? Les usually stops there for dinner or a beer before the game. I suppose he dumped extra tickets off on Charlie—I see some of the waitresses here every once in a while."

"Yeah, I stop by Charlie's place every now and then," Reddick said. "You think Charlie Hathaway had any reason to snuff old Lester?"

"Well . . ." Sussman ran the tape back slowly. "I doubt it, but maybe he saw something, who knows. I'll tell you what, Dwayne—let me borrow this tape for the afternoon, do you mind? I'd like to take it over to the studio and get a photocopy of this one frame here. Maybe I can find out who some of these people are."

Reddick raised his eyebrows. "Andy, my man, you aren't taking this investigation on yourself, are you?"

Sussman put the tape into reverse and watched as the basketball game sped back to the opening tap. "I've got a career to think of, Dwayne."

"Let it ride, man. They got nothing on you. They don't let you back in a few days, you sue." Reddick buttoned up a blue silk shirt and pulled a thick wool sweater over it. "Take a vacation, Andy, go someplace warm. Go to Florida for the week."

Sussman took the tape out of the video recorder, slipped it in its box, and stuck it in his briefcase. "I just want to look a few things over. See if I can pick out something obvious, maybe help things along."

"Yeah, well, be careful, Andrew. Don't flash the tape around; that detective's scrounging around the generator room, trying to find out who blew the fuses."

"He's there right now?"

Reddick pulled a heavy black winter coat out of his locker. "Andy, you're crazy, man. Go back home and go to sleep."

"Yeah, thanks, Dwayne." Sussman snapped the briefcase shut. "Take it easy, I'll see you tomorrow night."

"Later, Andrew."

Sussman left the locker room and walked through the maze of small passageways toward the maintenance center where the fuses were located. He had been there once before, several seasons ago, when a phone company screw-up had kept them off the air for an entire quarter. He had tailed the engineer, watching as he tested all the lines, but the man had become irritated, and Sussman had decided that the best policy in general, when dealing with problems of that nature, was to pop open a beer and study the stock quotations he hid under his game program.

Sussman approached the maintenance center, saw the small door half open, and stopped about fifty yards from the fuse boxes. He could see the angular figure of Detective Lafferty, wrapped in his trenchcoat, examining some loose wires. Beside Lafferty was a smaller man in a torn green T-shirt and a red windbreaker that read "Chicago Stadium." Sussman crept up about half the distance to the door and crouched behind a dingy-looking water cooler.

"Just a small timer," the man in the windbreaker was saying, "stuck onto a charge, size of a hockey puck."

"And nobody noticed?" the detective asked.

"Well, from the looks of the burn marks on the box here, it was put on the back side. It wasn't too big a charge, just enough to knock us out for a few minutes."

Detective Lafferty examined the charred fuse box for a couple of moments. "And who had access to this place?"

The electrician shrugged. "There's people going in and

out of here all the time. Building maintenance people, telephone people, TV and radio engineers—''

"Ouch!" said Andy Sussman, still crouched behind the water cooler. He had slipped in a small pool of water that was leaking from a pipe and banged his knee on the cement floor. He swore softly, then got up and flexed the knee a few times.

"Who's that?" coughed Lafferty, shuffling down the hallway. He stopped in front of the water cooler. "Mr. Sussman?"

"I was just trying to get a drink of water and I slipped." Sussman rubbed his knee, looked into Detective Lafferty's eyes, and saw the gaze of a gravely suspicious man. "Uh, actually, I was just in the locker room, talking to Dwayne Reddick, and he said you were down here."

"Who?"

"Reddick. One of the players? On the Flames?"

"Oh." Lafferty ran his hand over the floor below the water fountain. "And you have some business with me?"

"Well, yes, actually . . ." This was not going to be as easy as Murray Glick had suggested, Sussman thought.

"You come back here often, Mr. Sussman?"

"No, like I said, Detective, Dwayne told me you were here—"

"But you knew just where it was? You didn't have any trouble finding the place?"

Great, thought Sussman. The Perpetrator returning to the Scene of the Crime. "Detective Lafferty," he said, "I work in this building forty-two nights a year. I've been here three seasons now. Eventually, I learn where most everything is."

"Very interesting," coughed Lafferty, flipping the page of his notebook.

"Detective, look, I knew you were in the building, I

41

just thought you *might* want to talk to me about the case. I'm trying to be helpful."

Lafferty coughed again, stared at his notebook for a minute, then looked back up at Sussman. "No, Mr. Sussman. No, I don't think there's anything we need to be discussing right now."

"Well, then—"

"Thanks for offering though."

"You're welcome."

Detective Lafferty headed back toward the fuse boxes. "Oh, and Mr. Sussman," he said, turning around.

"Yes?"

"As long as you're in such a mood to be cooperative, how about making sure you stay around town for the next few days? Just in case we do need you, eventually?"

"Fine, I'd be happy to help, Detective. My number's in the book, you can call me any time."

"Good." Lafferty coughed again and stuck his notebook in his back pocket. "Good-bye, Mr. Sussman."

"*Ciao,*" mumbled Sussman. He stood frozen in the tiny hallway for a moment, balancing the briefcase on his hip. Then he slapped the water cooler with his palm, kicked at the puddle of water, and stalked back out to the parking lot.

6

"WE MISSED YOU at the funeral yesterday," said Wilfred P. Brandt, sitting at his massive oak desk, flanked by his attorney on one side and Detective Lafferty on the other.

"The funeral?"

"Lester Beldon's funeral."

"Yes, I know whose funeral it was."

"Frankly," said Wilfred P. Brandt, "we were shocked and disappointed at your failure to attend, Andy. Lester was a beloved member of the WCGO family. The entire office was there and we certainly expected you, who worked so closely with him—"

"Mr. Brandt," interrupted Susie Ettenger, "the fact is, you asserted yesterday that my client was the subject of an investigation relating to Lester Beldon's murder. Based on that, we felt it would be improper for him to attend the funeral, not to mention how upsetting it might be to the grieving family, the members of whom have Mr. Sussman's utmost sympathy."

Sussman folded his hands and smiled approvingly at Susie, wondering if her beautiful brown eyes and soft amber hair had the same tantalizing effect on Brandt and his attorney as they had on him. He supposed not. The attorney, a broad-shouldered man in his mid-fifties, was one of the Masons in the prestigious firm of Mason, Mason and

Prowse. He pursed his lips and furrowed his brow in Susie's direction; apparently the strength of their case was not yet great enough to warrant the actual utterance of a word.

"It seems to me," Susie continued, "that the image and reputation of WCGO is hardly helped when one of its most visible personalities is under suspicion of murder by his own management, particularly when such suspicion is totally groundless." Susie adjusted the slim tie she wore with her business suit. She was dressed conservatively today, a change from the breezy blouses and bright skirts that she wore for Sussman's contract-negotiating sessions. Susie's presence had had an insidiously wonderful effect on those meetings, drawing them out of Brandt's stuffy men's clubs, her charm and efficiency making Brandt squirm uncomfortably while WCGO's highest-paid women employees served them coffee. Today, though, Susie seemed dug in for corporate Armageddon, and Sussman couldn't blame her.

"I should point out," interjected Brandt, "that Mr. Sussman's suspension was based not on the murder, but on his unfortunate choice of words following the restoration of power after the blackout—"

"Mr. Brandt, my client sincerely regrets the language used following the discovery that his broadcasting partner had been shot in the back and was slumped in front of him, dead."

Andy Sussman tried to suppress a smirk. Something about stodgy old Wilfred Brandt seemed to encourage sarcasm, and he was happy to see it was not just in him.

"The point is," Susie said, catching herself, "whatever the reason for your action, the *perception* of the public, *your* public, Mr. Brandt, will be that my client's suspension is directly related to Lester Beldon's murder. That, it seems to me, is not good publicity for WCGO."

Wilfred P. Brandt nodded and cracked a smile. "We're pleased to know that Mr. Sussman has the best interests of WCGO at heart, Miss Ettenger. Unfortunately, certain facts, as described to us this morning by Detective Lafferty, implore us to take a cautious path. Detective?"

Detective Laffert looked toward the lawyer for approval, then cleared his throat "Gentlemen, Miss, uh . . ."

"Ettenger," snapped Susie.

"Miss Ettenger, as I was explaining to Mr. Brandt and Mr. Mason, your client and I had a previous meeting this morning. It seems Mr. Sussman was snooping around the scene of the crime—"

"Not 'snooping,' " Sussman said. "I thought I explained that rather clearly—"

"Eavesdropping, would you say?"

"Detective Lafferty, I was told exactly where you were, I was looking for *you.*"

"That's an interesting explanation, Mr. Sussman, and it may be true. Another interpretation might be that you were concerned about the direction the investigation was taking."

"I *am* concerned about the direction the investigation is taking—"

"Detective Lafferty," said Susie Ettenger, "are you charging Mr. Sussman with a crime?"

"Not at this time, ma'am."

"Are you suggesting that his presence in a building where he works forty-two nights a year somehow implicates him in a murder which he had no cause or method to commit?"

"Miss Ettenger—"

"Detective Lafferty, have you received ballistics reports and autopsy reports from the police lab yet?"

"We got them back yesterday—"

"And is there anything in those reports, Detective Lafferty, to lead you to the conclusion that Mr. Sussman was in any way involved in the death of Mr. Beldon?"

The room fell silent for a moment, until Wilfred P. Brandt nodded in the direction of the detective.

"Gentlemen . . . and ladies," Lafferty said, "we don't have the specifics down on this crime yet. What we do know is that whoever was involved had to have knowledge of and access to the complicated workings inside the Stadium. They had to know where Lester Beldon would be and how to get onto the floor so they could get into position to shoot him, and how to get off the premises before the power went back on. We haven't been able to pinpoint who that person or persons might be, but certainly Mr. Sussman meets many of the qualifications—"

"So do at least a hundred other people," said Susie. "Including all the members of the basketball team, the officials, the maintenance employees, and at least nine or ten employees of WCGO. Mr. Brandt, have you taken any action against any other of your employees who were at the Stadium that night?"

"That action will all be taken in due course," interrupted the attorney Mason.

Mason speaks, thought Sussman. Score one for Susie.

"I don't believe the time passed has been sufficient for making judgments on all my client's employees," Mason continued. "However, in the case of Mr. Sussman, given his behavior on the night of the incident, his long-standing attitude toward Mr. Beldon, and the revelations of Detective Lafferty, we feel it would be appropriate to continue our action pending further investigative results."

Susie Ettenger looked at her legal pad, then calmly folded it up and stuck it into her portfolio. "All right, Mr. Mason, let me make our position clear then: My client had nothing whatsoever to do with the unfortunate death of Lester Beldon. We consider this a deliberate and malicious attempt to slander his good name, restrict his livelihood, and damage his career. The law firm of Chavous and Birnbaum has every intention of seeking swift and complete restitution for all damages done to Mr. Sussman's reputation, in regard to your suspension scheduled to begin tomorrow night. Do I make myself clear?''

"It always grieves me to hear that one of our family here at WCGO feels he's been mistreated," said Wilfred P. Brandt. "I hope this won't affect future relations—"

"We understand your position," broke in Mason, rising from his seat. "And you can be assured we'll give it our greatest attention. Now, if no one has anything else to bring up . . ."

No one did, and a few minutes later Andy Sussman was standing in the lobby outside WCGO's offices, drawing up battle plans with Susie Ettenger for the next round.

"So much for reconciliatory strategy," Susie said, her portfolio tucked underneath her arm.

"It was a nice try," said Sussman. "Not that it's any different than any other of the hassles we've had with them."

"I just thought I could get you back on the air without a protracted struggle. The thing is, Andy, given what I think their disposition is toward you at the moment, they might be willing to lose a little money, just to, uh . . ."

"Screw me?"

"Something along that order, yes."

Sussman made a tentative effort to put his arm around Susie's shoulder, then drew back. "Well, anyway, we went toe to toe with Mason, Mason and Prowse. One of the Masons, anyway. I'm proud of you, kid."

Susie Ettenger looked at Sussman cockeyed.

All right, Sussman thought, shoving his hand in his pocket, I didn't mean to sound patronizing. He had to admit, though, that he'd felt an emotional attachment to Susie as she stood up to Brandt and Mason and the cop. He wondered if he had any business feeling defensive for her, protective about someone that, after all, was supposed to be protecting him. If he really believed she was such an underdog, maybe he should have someone else representing him. His career *was* on the line, after all.

"This isn't a game, Andy," Susie said, softly. "We don't get any moral victories for hanging in tough."

"Moral victories? Hanging in tough? Sounds like you've been reading the sports pages lately." (Or listening to my broadcasts, Sussman thought. That would be the day.)

Susie shrugged. "I just want you to know, if you have any doubts about my capabilities, feel free to find someone else to represent you. You can call Irv Chavous, I don't mind. He might take the case personally."

"I don't have any doubts, Susie, really." Sussman realized that what he actually wanted to do was ask Susie out to dinner. He wasn't quite sure how to go about it, but he guessed that firing her as his attorney was not a good way to start.

"Look," Susie said, "there's my ride. Think about it and call me back, okay? I'll be at the office all day tomorrow and Saturday." She waved at a tall man in a beige overcoat who was standing by the lobby doorway, pointing at a car that was double-parked.

"Hey, no problem, Suse. Really, everything went great. I don't need Irv Chavous."

"All right then. I'm going to try and get a copy of Lafferty's police reports—we have a right to see them, if they have anything to do with your involvement in the case."

"Fine."

"And stay away from that detective, Andy. All you're doing is making him more suspicious."

Susie was drifting away now, toward the man in the overcoat. Boyfriend? Sussman wondered. Law partner? Both?

"Keep your cool, okay?" she shouted. "Maybe stay away from the Stadium for a couple of days. We'll be in touch."

"Gotcha, Susie." Sussman waved good-bye. "Talk to you in a day or two."

Susie Ettenger smiled and waved back. Then she handed her portfolio to the man in the beige overcoat, put her arm around his waist, and headed out through the revolving doors, disappearing into the rush-hour crowd.

7

"ONE TAPE?" SAID Murray Glick, scooping the nuts off a hot-fudge sundae with his little white plastic spoon. "That's all you got for me, Hoops, one tape? Where's the ballistics report and the last day itinerary?"

"Chrissakes, Murray, the stuff's not exactly available on demand." Sussman crunched the last of a chocolate-mint ice-cream cone and licked the remains off his fingers. "Everytime I get near that Detective Lafferty, he looks like he's getting ready to fit me for a hood."

"Ahh, lighten up, Hoops. They haven't executed anyone in this state in years." Murray slurped down a maraschino cherry. "What's this, what's this picture?"

"That's a blow-up from Dwayne's videotape. It's from the first half, you can see some of the people who were sitting right behind us."

Glick took the picture and held it up to his desk lamp. "Charlie Hathaway, I recognize him. He's thinking of putting a restaurant in here, you know that, Hoops?"

"He may have to change his clientele a little."

"Hathaway's North. He'll be right down there on the first floor, across from Neiman-Marcus. Who's this guy?" Murray squinted at the photocopy. "I've seen this guy somewhere, Hoops. He ring a bell to you?"

Sussman took the picture and eyed a slightly built man

with a mustache. The man was in his early thirties, or so it seemed from the grainy picture, and he was wearing a dark ski jacket and a stocking cap.

"It gets hot in there during a game, doesn't it?" Murray said, unloosening his own collar. "Course, I'm only there when the crowd's big, lots of body heat, but still. When was this taken?"

"End of the second quarter; two-twenty left."

"Seems to me he'd be pretty hot, unless he just got there." Murray wiped his mouth with a paper napkin. "Or unless he's getting ready to leave. I want to check this picture out, Hoops, let me hold on to it."

"Why don't you just keep the tape?"

"Right." Murray took Sussman's videocassette and was inserting it in his Betamax when the phone rang. "Hang on, Hoops, commerce beckons. Hello?" he said into the phone. "Mrs. Brenner, have I got wonderful news for you!" Murray opened his desk drawer and pulled out a notebook that had several store catalogs stuffed inside. "Okay, Mrs. Brenner, got a pencil? Good . . . there's a beautiful cashmere sweater over at Justins, light brown, medium, it's on sale all week. . . . Yes, I know it's his fiftieth birthday. . . . We also picked out a gold-plated ice bucket and tongs at Neiman-Marcus, with highball glasses and a gold-plated mixer. Yes, Mrs. Brenner, it's very elegant; believe me, I'd love to have it myself. . . . April sixteenth, Mrs. Brenner, I'll be thirty-two. Thanks, Mrs. Brenner, you're an angel. I'll send you the bill. Bye, now."

"There are eight million cases in the Naked City," Sussman said, as Murray hung up the phone.

"Don't knock it, Hoops. I can get life insurance now, did I tell you that?" Murray flicked on his VCR, ran it at fast forward, then reversed it to the beginning. "What's this?'' he asked, as Lester Beldon's corpulent smile flashed on the screen.

"That's Lester's halftime show."

"At the beginning of the game?"

Sussman sharpened the focus. "Lester does—did—a halftime show for the cable network and for WCGO-TV, when they televised road games. He recorded his interview before the game, and they played it at halftime."

"Hmm. Let's take a look."

Murray started the tape again and turned up the volume. There was Lester Beldon, all 210 pounds of him, about twenty of them hanging out of his Hawaiian shirt and tumbling over his baggy slacks. The portable TV lights reflected off Lester's dyed blond hair and showed up as tiny dots on the lenses of his aviator glasses. He was standing at courtside, just in front of the broadcasting table, a lavaliere mike stuck to his lapel. He was interviewing Hugh Delaney, an advance scout for the Boston Celtics. Glick stopped the tape just as Beldon began his interview.

"See something?" asked Sussman.

"Just taking inventory, Andrew." Murray scribbled a few notes down on a scratch pad. "What's that on the table?"

"Just the pregame stats. The briefcase is mine, the clipboard is Lester's."

"The leopard-skin chair?"

"Whose do you think?"

"The overcoat?"

"His."

Glick peered at the picture, scanning the empty seats in back of the table.

"It's an hour before game time, Murray. Nobody's there yet."

Glick turned the tape back on.

"I'm here with Hugh Delaney," Lester Beldon was

saying, with a broad grin, "assistant coach and superscout for the Boston Celtics. Hugh, good to see you again, old buddy!"

"Pleasure to be here, Les," Delaney mumbled.

"Hugh, you're one of the all-time greats, of course, back in your days with the Pistons and the Cincinnati Royals—I was with the St. Louis Hawks, then, my rookie season, as a matter of fact. I can still remember it: my coach, good old Charlie Simms, bless his soul, he looked at me and he said, 'Beldon, can you guard number eighteen out there?' And of course, being a rookie and wanting to get off the bench, I said 'Sure!' and Charlie sent me into the game, and old number eighteen, I'll tell you what, folks, he proceeded to burn me for about thirty points in one half, right Hugh?"

"Yes, sir, Les, that Tommy Rogers was quite a shot—I used to guard him in practice all the time—"

"No, Hugh—I was talking about you, buddy."

"Well, Les, I was number twenty-eight, actually. Tommy Rogers was eighteen. You were probably guarding him, unless it was December, when he hurt his knee—"

"No, Hugh, it was definitely you, the old Dipper."

"J.C. Curtis was number eight, he had a terrific hook shot. It could have been him—"

"No, Hugh, I'm positive—"

"Well, maybe, there was a mix-up. One night in Fort Wayne, Les, someone broke into the locker room and stole all our uniforms. Someone had to run into town and get some T-shirts, otherwise we would have had to play shirts and skins."

"Heh, heh, heh," chortled Les Beldon, his belly bubbling inside the Hawaiian shirt. "That would have been quite a sight, Hugh."

Andy Sussman flicked the tape off. "Well, there you have it, Murray, the quintessential Les Beldon interview."

Glick rolled the tape ahead at fast speed, looking for any intrusions in the picture, but nobody else appeared. "You say he did one of these every night, Hoops?"

"Yeah. It was pretty amazing. I've never seen anyone with the capacity to screw up so consistently—"

"I want to see 'em."

Sussman rolled his eyes. "What, the interviews?"

"Yeah."

"*All* of them?"

"Can you do that, Hoops?"

"Well, I suppose. . . ." Sussman was not crazy about raiding the WCGO tape library and did not know if he had access to the pay-TV service that did the home games. On the other hand, there were Dwayne Reddick's tapes, if he kept them that far back.

"Get them, Hoops, bring 'em to me by Saturday."

"Did you see something?"

"Can't tell yet. Now, how about your homework on Beldon's personal life." Murray pulled a *Time* magazine from his desk drawer. On the cover was the headline, "Athletes and Drugs: A Special Report." "Was he involved in any of this, Andy?"

Sussman laughed. "Lester? Gimme a break, Murray, the guy never had anything stronger than a shot and a beer."

"Not to your knowledge, that is."

"Not to anyone's knowledge."

Murray spooned out the remains of his hot-fudge sundae. "Hoops, listen. You remember when I was helping clear Sly Thomas last year on that statutory rape thing? I found out a few things that didn't have anything to do with the investigation."

"About *Lester?*"

54

"About Sly."

"Look, Murray, I think it was generally understood that Sly had a few problems back then, but he's clean now."

"You're sure?"

"Well I can't *prove* it. But what does that have to do with Lester Beldon?"

"Who knows? All I'm saying is, the stuff's around, you can't ignore it. Now, what about Lester's debts? What about his home life?"

"I have no idea, Murray."

Murray reached into his cigar canister, pulled out a Don Diego, and tamped the end on his blotter. "Well, maybe we'd better find out."

"I've only had two days, Murray."

"You're doing a fine job, pal, believe me. Now how about the police info?"

"Susie Ettenger said she'd get it for me. We're entitled to it, supposedly, if they're going to press any charges."

"Ah, Susie!" Glick lit his cigar and blew a smoke ring across the room. "You called her, Hoops. Good for you. Did you offer to split the settlement with her and move to Dominique?"

"Not yet, Murray. I thought I'd wait until the damages were awarded and then just sort of surprise her."

"Don't wait too long, Hoops. Make your move. I'll tell you, girls like that, once they get close to the old three-0—they may talk about how great their career is and everything, but once they find their Mr. Right . . . *WHAM-O!* Like a rock, Andrew."

"I'll try and expedite things, Murray."

"What about Wendy Altman, you still after her ass?"

"Watch your mouth, Murray, we're talking about Lorraine and Irv Altman's little girl."

"Yeah, yeah, I saw her in the mall the other day, juggling about thirteen packages. She could barely see ahead of her. She looked like that statue you see in the court-room, you know, Blind Justice, with Neiman-Marcus bags on one side of the scale and Lord and Taylor on the other.''

"Did you say hello?"

"I waved. I was at the popcorn stand, I don't think she saw me. I think you'd better watch it with that girl, Hoops."

"Thanks, Murray."

Glick turned off the power on his video recorder and took the tape out of the machine. "I can keep this for a few days?"

"Sure, Murray."

"I'll check it against my files and call you if anything turns up."

"Right, Mur."

Glick cuffed Sussman on the shoulder. "Hang in there, Hoops. We're hot on the trail."

"Gotcha, Murray." Andy Sussman patted Murray on the back and snatched one of his Don Diego cigars from the leather canister. Then he left Murray's office, waved to the secretary, and wandered back into the translucent haze of Northbrook Court.

8

ON FRIDAY NIGHT, when the Chicago Flames were playing the Indiana Pacers in their fifty-sixth game of the season, Andy Sussman went to the Chicago Symphony with Wendy Altman. He did it partly to stay away from Detective Lafferty; partly to prove to Wendy Altman that he was not such a schmuck, after all—she *had* gotten tickets several weeks in advance, even if she hadn't bothered to check the Flames' schedule first ("They won't give you a night off to see the *symphony* instead of a dumb basketball game?"); and partly because he wanted to get laid, a possibility he viewed with mixed emotions—he wanted to keep his relationship with this girl at a distance, but if he was going to sit through three hours of classical music, he certainly deserved it. In any case, Sussman was not completely cut off from the basketball game. He had brought a transistor radio along with him and hidden it in the pocket of his sport coat, along with a tiny earphone that ran up his left arm.

Sussman settled back, his right arm around Wendy, and raised his left arm to his ear. He had been wondering what turkey WCGO had gotten to replace him for tonight's broadcast, and it had turned out to be Paul Wendell, a cloying, nasal-sounding deejay who did the "Big Band Cavalcade of Memories" every Sunday afternoon.

"There's Reddick with the—no wait, that was Bryce," Wendell stumbled. Sussman heard a whistle, then a few boos from the crowd. "Wait, the Indianas have it now, let's see, Thomas—he passes out of bounds, it's the Flames' ball, and I think there's a foul on—no wait, Long throws it inbounds to Reddick, he passes to, wait a second . . . and, there's a basket—" Sussman turned off the radio.

"Oh, isn't this wonderful," said Wendy Altman, as the song, or movement, or whatever it was, ended. Sussman started to applaud, then noticed that he was the only one clapping as the orchestra immediately proceeded into the next movement.

"Wait 'til it's over," Wendy whispered.

"I just liked that last note," Sussman said. "You know, the way they all ended together?" Wendy elbowed him in the ribs, and he slunk into his seat. At least you knew when a basketball game ended, he thought. They rang a buzzer.

When the concert was over, Sussman slipped into the washroom, unrigged his earphone, and glanced through the program to see what it was he was supposed to have listened to. A few minutes later he was escorting Wendy across the Loop to Hathaway's Pub on Dearborn Street, for their postconcert drinks and conversation.

"I don't suppose you could have found someplace a little more elegant?" Wendy said, lifting the edge of her pink, ankle-length down coat as she walked beneath the frayed canopy overhanging the entrance to Hathaway's.

"You said to pick any bar I wanted. Here, look, they were at the concert, too." Sussman pointed to a middle-aged couple who were standing near the musty wooden bar, underneath the black-and-white photographs autographed by various Chicago athletes. Tourists, he thought. He could imagine the dog-eared pages in their Fodor's

Chicago guidebook: "For that real Windy City atmosphere, don't miss Hathaway's Pub in the heart of the Loop. Enjoy the Town's most complete list of imported beers amidst an earthy Chicago atmosphere."

"Hey, Sussman!" said a raspy voice, coming from a dimly lit alcove by the front door. "Whatsa matter, they got you red-shirted tonight?" It was Charlie Hathaway, the proprietor. He was dressed in a powder-blue seersucker suit, with suspenders holding his pants up over a nearly bursting crotch. A thick cigar was welded to his mouth. "Chrissakes, Sussman, I don't mind you take a night off, but go to Vegas or something. Go to Miami, get warm." He wrapped an arm around Wendy. "Just kidding, beautiful, delighted to have you here."

"Our pleasure," Wendy said stiffly.

"Say, Charlie," Sussman said, waving away some cigar smoke that seemed to have formed a stationary front just ahead of his eyeballs. "Can you—"

"Just a second, Suss." Hathaway waddled over to the coat check closet, where a muscular-looking black man in a leather jacket was arguing with the hatcheck girl.

"It's the beret, sister, it's sittin' right there on the shelf."

"I'm sorry, sir, that's on number one-fifty-three—you're one-twenty-eight."

"Your mama! Gimme that hat—"

"What's going on?" demanded Hathaway, plodding over to the dusty cloakroom.

"Hey, man, lemme have my *hat!* I come in here for a coupla beers, it's costin' me thirty bucks—"

"Trudy, babe, give the man his hat."

"It's not on his number, Mr. Hathaway."

"Trudy!"

The hatcheck girl swore under her breath, slapped the

beret in the man's hand, and retreated to the back of the closet.

"Criminy," muttered Charlie Hathaway, returning to Sussman and Wendy. He led them back through the smoke, to a small wooden table that was adorned with a set of chipped salt and pepper shakers, a tin napkin holder, and a basket of popcorn. "Think a good hatcheck girl's not important? Mine quit last night, look what happens. Ran off with some comedian, he's gonna be on Johnny Carson, he tells her. Fat chance." He wiped off the table with a filthy towel and signaled for a waitress. "Stay outta the restaurant business," he whispered into Sussman's ear, "it'll break your heart."

A few moments later a waitress came along, a tall, bosomy blonde, dressed in black lace panty hose and a black miniskirt. Sussman ordered a double Scotch for himself and a glass of chardonnay for Wendy, then watched as she pulled out her compact and retraced her pink lipstick. There was no doubt that Wendy was an attractive girl. She had strawberry blond hair—not natural, Sussman knew, having known her since grade school, but it looked good on her. Blue eyes, a pert nose. She looked after herself: tennis, when it was popular, now jogging. A nice body. Still, there was something about Wendy Altman that made Sussman reluctant to get too close. She was like the furniture in his mother's living room: beautiful, well maintained and expensive, but not for him to touch. Sussman was not sure what would happen if he ever got as far as taking Wendy to bed. He just could not visualize her naked. He expected to take off her clothes and find her body wrapped in plastic covering, with a little tag on it that said, "Do not remove under penalty of law."

"Andy," said Wendy, putting away her compact, "do you mind if I ask you a personal question?"

What am I supposed to say to that? Sussman thought.

Yes, I mind. I don't like my conversations to rise above the level of general banality. "Sure, go ahead."

"Andy, aren't you getting kind of tired of going to basketball games all the time? I mean, I know every kid wants to get involved with sports, but you're thirty-two years old now—"

"Thirty-one and a half."

"Oh, well that's different."

Sussman sighed. "Wendy," he said, "does the word 'career' mean anything to you?"

"Career, as in business, or law?"

"Career as in sports journalism, which happens to compensate me quite adequately right now. Which pays for a condominium in Lincoln Park, and a Datsun 260Z, and a full membership at the East Bank Club. Do you know what the top people in my field make, Wendy? Howard Cosell, Brent Musburger, Dick Enberg?"

"I thought everybody hated Howard Cosell."

"Twenty million people hated him, every Monday night. You know what that breaks down to, per hate?"

"Andy." Wendy took Sussman's hand and caressed it by the ring finger, then pushed it away. "Oh, Andy . . ."

"Oh, Andy, what?"

"That's not what I mean. You've got to understand, it's not the—" Wendy reached for the napkin and coughed.

"Not the what?" Not the money? Would she say it?

"Andy, is there a ladies' room in this place?"

No fair, Sussman thought, she's calling time-out. "Right to the left," he said, "behind the bar."

Wendy walked off to the ladies' room. As soon as she was out of sight, Sussman stood up and waved at Charlie Hathaway, who was back at the front door, lecturing the hatcheck girl.

"Just a second," Hathaway growled.

Sussman waved again.

"What?" shouted Hathaway, trundling over. "I got waitresses here, ya know. I don't need to bring the drinks myself."

"This is business."

"Oh, yeah?"

Sussman cleared his throat. "Charlie . . ."

"What?"

"Charlie, sit."

Hathaway sat.

"All right, Charlie, I need some information. You were at the game Tuesday night, when Lester Beldon was murdered, right?"

Hathaway popped a kernel of popcorn into his mouth. "How'd you know that?"

Sussman pulled the grainy photocopy out of his coat pocket and held it in front of Hathaway. "That you?"

"So it is. What is this, Suss, 'Candid Camera'?"

"Charlie, this is important. I need to know what you saw Tuesday night."

"What I saw?" Hathaway spread a cloud of cigar smoke into the foul air. "I saw Lester Beldon get his ass blown away, that's what I saw."

"You *saw* it?"

"I didn't *see* it, it was dark. I saw it afterward, just like you. Whatsamatter, Andy, you in some kind of trouble?"

"Who's this guy?" Sussman said, pointing at the man in the ski jacket and stocking cap.

"I dunno."

"You've never seen him before?"

"I ain't seen him in here, Andy, and if I ain't seen him in here, I probably ain't seen him anywhere."

"Okay, Charlie, let's back up. Did you see Lester Beldon the night of the game? Did he come in here?"

"Sure, he comes in before every game. After, too."

"Tell me what he did, as precisely as you can remember."

"Geez, slow down, Andy." Hathaway gnawed at his cigar. "Whatta they got the chair all wired up for you already?"

A waitress came by with the drinks for Sussman and Wendy. Sussman took a sip from his Scotch and stared at Hathaway.

"What does he do, Suss? He does what he always does. Walks in in his neon suit, takes a table, orders a bottle of some foreign beer he can't pronounce, asks who needs tickets—"

"He had extra tickets that night?"

"Yeah, how do you think I got in? You think I'd pay to see those losers?"

"How many tickets did he give away that night, Charlie?"

Hathaway gave a baggy-eyed, walrus shrug. "Six, seven, who knows? He left 'em on the bar, first come, first served."

"So who went, do you remember?"

"Jesus, Andy. . . ." Hathaway thought for a moment. "Ah, Arnie, one of the bartenders, went, I think—took along a friend or two, maybe. See, the tickets aren't all together, so I can't exactly say. I just took two for myself, called my nephew up and brought him over. Nice kid, Andy, twelve years old, a big sports fan. It was a sad thing for a kid to see, what happened."

"I'm sure, Charlie."

"Poor dumb Lester—who the fuck would want to shoot him? Ever met anybody more harmless?" Hathaway started to rise, then turned and whispered to Sussman. "Hey, Andy, you don't think . . ."

"What, Charlie?"

"You don't think they were aiming for you, do ya?"

"Me?"

"Yeah, well, you know. You rub a few people the wrong way, so I'm told. Nothing personal, just what I hear. Maybe some rookie got cut, some player's wife didn't like the way you been treatin' her old man. Maybe the lights go out, they get a little crazy."

Sussman pondered the thought for a moment, but could not possibly imagine anyone mistaking Lester Beldon in his pink Hawaiian shirt for himself, even in the dark. "I don't think so, Charlie."

"Maybe you better hire someone, watch your rear for a while. I got bouncers'll do that for some extra pocket money."

"Thanks for the thought, Charlie. Listen, do me a favor, will you? Think about Tuesday night. If you remember anything—"

"Am I interrupting something?" asked Wendy, returning from the ladies' room.

"Mr. Sussman, a pleasure as usual to have you gracing the premises." Hathaway got up and wiped off the seat. "Pardon me, ma'am, enjoy your wine."

Wendy remained standing as Hathaway walked away, then stared at the seat for a moment, as if Hathaway's massive rear had made it unsuitable for her own finely sculpted bottom. "Andy," she said, "I'm feeling a little, uh . . . queasy. I think that cigar smoke got to me. Do you think you could take me home?"

Sussman took the folded photocopy and stuck it in his pocket. "Sure, that's okay. We could go back to my place for a drink, if you want. We could finish discussing my future."

"That's okay, Andy. Just home, if it's not too much trouble."

"All right." Sussman left seven dollars to cover the bill and tip, then helped Wendy with her coat. Safe, he thought. Safe to go to basketball games again. Safe to concentrate his amorous attentions on Susie Ettenger. Unless, he thought, he really, seriously wanted to get laid. He could take Wendy home, apologize for taking her to Hathaway's, express his true love and willingness to grow and oh, Wendy, you have the most beautiful eyes . . .

"See you, Suss," said Charlie Hathaway, as Sussman walked out the door. "Take care of yourself. Remember what I said. CYA."

"Right, Charlie."

"CYA?" asked Wendy, as they walked down Dearborn Street. "What does that mean, Andy?"

"Cover your ass," said Sussman. He gave Wendy a playful pat on hers, but Wendy pushed his hand away, and Sussman walked her silently back to the car, tabling his salacious intentions for the night.

9

It was Sunday morning, a warmish day for February; little rivulets of dirty water trickled off the humpbacked snowbanks on Fullerton Avenue and bled into the street, washing into sewers or down into the newborn potholes that were exposed through the melted ice and slush. Sussman was driving to De Paul University, where the Flames practiced when the hockey team was using the Stadium, which was most of the time. He parked his Datsun on the street alongside Alumni Hall, the tiny De Paul gym nestled underneath the el tracks, and walked inside.

"Andrew, my man," shouted Dwayne Reddick, breathing hard as he ran laps around the court. "I got your package. Let me finish my wind sprints, then we've got a chalk talk, then I'll be right with you." Without breaking stride, he scooped a basketball from a cart that stood by the benches and whipped a pass at Sussman. "Practice your jumper, Andy, we might have to suit you up."

Sussman caught the ball in his stomach and set his coat down on the folding bleacher seats, which were pushed up like an accordion. Reddick and Cliff Bennett, another forward, were the only starting players left on the floor. The rest of the players had headed for the locker room, with the exception of Sly Thomas, who was standing against the far basket standard, having an animated conversation with a woman.

Sussman had given up trying to keep track of Sly's coterie of female companions, most of whom showed no hesitation to visit practices and hold running conversations with Sly about the state of their relationships. This girl happened to be white, with long red hair that flowed down to her waist. She wore a dirty white overcoat which she had unbuttoned but not taken off, despite the steamy conditions in the gym, and she was holding a small suitcase. Sussman waved at Sly, who scowled back and turned the girl around so that she faced the leather-padded basket support. They continued their argument, the woman repeatedly jabbing Sly's belly, Sly waving his hands in a plea for divine understanding.

"Hey, Andy," interrupted a wispy voice.

Sussman felt Señor Flame's bony fingers tapping on his shoulder and turned around. "G'morning, Señor," he said. Señor Flame was, to Sussman's knowledge, the only team mascot in the NBA who showed up for Sunday morning practices. He was dressed in his mangy orange-and-blue Flame suit, which was unzipped in the front so that Sussman could see his face and shoulders.

"I want to show you something, Andy, okay? You give me your opinion?" Señor Flame had a narrow face with a pencil-thin mustache and a receding hairline. Dwarfed by his Flame suit, he looked scrawny and slightly fragile. "I gotta new routine, Andy. The doc says I gotta take the pressure off the knee, no more spins, no more twisting when I dance. Hey, I miss two games already, you know? I gotta get back in action, before they put me on injured reserve, maybe find somebody else."

Back underneath the basket, Sly Thomas's girlfriend had hit him in the chest with her suitcase and was stalking away. "You watch your mouth, woman," Sly shouted, then lowered his voice, in a tone barely audible to Sussman. "You stay away from here, baby. You wanna scream, you go scream at Bobby for a while."

Señor Flame poked Sussman in the shoulder. "You gotta play with the small hurts, right, Andy?" He adjusted his knee brace, then zipped up his uniform. "You watch this, okay?"

Sussman observed Sly's girlfriend leaving the gym as Sly hurried downstairs. "Okay, Señor," he said.

"Now we got the organ playin', right? Try and pretend you hear the organ. It's playin' 'We Got Fire in Our Eyes'—that's a hot number, Andy, you know that song?"

"Sounds familiar, Señor—hum a few bars."

Señor Flame took three steps forward, then pirouetted on his good knee. "We got fi-i-ire, in our eyes," he sang. "We got fi-i-ire, we got fi-i-ire, in our souls." He hopped on his good leg, whirled his hands around like a sorcerer, and jiggled his fingers at Sussman. "We're the flames of insurrection, we're the agents of destruction . . ." He stopped his dance. "It's the hands, you see Andy? I got to compensate for the lack of lateral movement, so I increased the hand motion. What do you think, man?"

"Inspired choreography, Señor. Maybe you should try out for 'Dance Fever' or the Rockettes."

"You think so?" Señor Flame peeled off his uniform, revealing a pair of dirty jeans and a T-shirt that read "Ferdy's Tacos." "I don't know, Andy. My bum knee and all, maybe it's too late for that. Señor Flame's maybe the best I can do, you know?"

Sussman patted Señor Flame's sloping shoulders. "Well, you hang in there, Señor." He noticed that Reddick and Bennett had left the floor, and the gym was now empty. "Señor, are you going to soak that knee?"

"Yeah, but I gotta wait 'til the players are done."

"Let's take a walk down, I think they're almost

through." Sussman put an arm around Señor Flame's waist and helped him negotiate the stairs down to the locker room. When they reached the entrance, he saw the players gathered around an open space in front of the lockers, listening to their coach, Ted Weaver, and a small, foreign-looking man in a gray sport jacket and slacks.

"You must be in a comple-e-e-tely relaxed state of mind to realize your full potential on the court," the man was saying, in an East Indian accent. "All-l-l the muscles in your legs, all-l-l the muscles in your arms are comple-e-e-tely relaxed. Your upper chest is relaxed . . . your breathing is deeeep and relaxed. . . ."

"I be any more relaxed, I be asleep out there," said Sly Thomas, cleaning his teeth with a toothpick. "How'm I supposed to thrill the crowd when I'm asleep?"

"Save it, Thomas," said Jack Bryce, the center. He was leaning forward over the bench, trying to concentrate on the speaker. "Try listening to someone besides yourself for a change. Maybe you'll hit the rim once in a while—I bet that'd give the crowd a thrill."

"Up your ass, Bryce."

"Now, now," said the East Indian man, in his sing-songy voice. "We need to let all our hostilities flow out. Hostility prevents us from reaching our full potential on the court. Now let's all take a deeeep breath. . . ."

Fifteen players and coaches breathed in at once, in a maneuver Sussman was certain would cause the walls of the tiny locker room to cave in.

"Now breathe out, and out goes the hostilities, out goes the anger. You are feeling much more relaxed, you are so-o-o-o relaxed, you are ready to play up to your full capabilities."

"I be up to my capabilities already," Sly Thomas said.

"Let's hope not," muttered Coach Weaver.

"Excuse me," said Señor Flame, tiptoeing to the edge of

69

the meeting. "If it's all right, I'm going to use the whirlpool for a few minutes, as long as everybody's out here."

"You have an injury?" inquired the little Indian man. "You are part of the team?"

"He's the mascot," muttered Bryce.

"Sorry," said Señor Flame, casting a jealous eye on the whirlpool. "I gotta bad knee."

"You try relaxation therapy first, before you try water jets. My name is Doctor Rav Kamurassi. I help you organize your mind and body." He turned to the rest of the team. "Now I teach you meditation, people. It is one very good way of relaxation. Some of you have already tried this, I understand."

"Yes, Doctor Kamurassi," said Bryce, "I've been leading TM seminars for the last couple of weeks."

"Yeah, you been havin' a great effect," said Sly Thomas. "You got three rebounds last night, you really reachin' your full potential, Bryce."

"Hey, Thomas, if this is too much for your attention span—"

"People, people," interrupted Doctor Kamurassi. "Meditation can be helpful to anyone. We need to reach full potential as a team as well as individuals. Now. . . . Mr. Thomas? Is that right?"

"You can call me Sly, baby."

"Okay, Mr. Sly. We are going to teach you meditation. We are going to help you choose a mantra."

"How 'bout just givin' me a back rub?"

"Your mantra is the word you repeat when you meditate, Mr. Sly. It will help you relax."

"I *am* relaxed, Doc. I don't need no word. I just need a gorgeous blonde, maybe one o' them new cheerleaders."

"Even that is better with meditation, Mr. Sly. Now I want you to think of a word. A word that completely relaxes you. A word that cuts off the outside world and makes you totally passive to everything around you."

"I ain't got any words like that," Sly said.

"How about 'defense'?" someone suggested.

"Up *yours!*" shouted Sly, looking for the offender. It was Dwayne Reddick.

"Excuse me, Doctor Kamurassi," said Reddick, shooting an icy glare at Thomas. "I've got to do a quick interview with our main radio man, here. Could you excuse me for a minute?"

Dr. Kamurassi started to protest, then stopped as Reddick stood to the full length of his six feet eight inches, 210 pounds. It was common knowledge that Dwayne Reddick would never so much as jostle anyone in anger, but no one was anxious to test the theory.

"Andrew, you're serious about all this, aren't you?" Reddick said, as he led Sussman to his cubicle.

"I told you, Dwayne, I can't wait around for those clowns at the police department to clear things up."

"Yeah, right." Reddick pulled an overnight bag full of videotapes out of his locker. "Here, these go all the way back." Reddick switched on his VCR. "I'll tell you what, though; you ought to tell those dudes at 'CGO to take that candy-assed job of theirs and stick it where the sun don't shine."

"I'm afraid the timing's not quite right for that, pal. And I'm too old to go to law school." Sussman watched the video monitor. It was showing the Phoenix game, in which Lester Beldon had been shot. "Jeez, Dwayne, you got that same tape on again?"

"We play at Phoenix next week, Andy. I gotta guard Eric Williams, he's a tough sucker. Here, you can see Sly's shot again." Reddick turned the sound up as Thomas went up for his pre-blackout jumper. For the thousandth time, Sussman saw Sly release his shot, heard the crowd gasp, saw the lights go out.

"Hey, Dwayne," Sussman said, perking his ears, "did you tape this from the networks?"

"Naw, Andy, I told you on the phone, I called the cable TV people. They sent me all these copies."

"So it's all live, no dubbing?"

"Yeah."

"Listen to this." Sussman wound the tape back, then started it again. The announcer called Thomas's dribble, then, as Sly went up to shoot, there was an audible crowd reaction. It was the same reaction Sussman had heard on the television version of the tape when he was watching the news, but he had assumed the noise was just random dubbing. "Did you hear that, Dwayne?"

Reddick shrugged. "Someone cheered, what about it?"

"Not someone, a whole bunch of people. Why would they start cheering just as Sly Thomas shoots?"

"Well, you know Sly, he always gets a reaction."

"In the middle of the third quarter, when we're fifteen points behind?"

Reddick looked cockeyed at Sussman.

"Dwayne, something happened out there. The crowd must have seen something, or someone. This is right before the blackout, remember? Right before someone went down to the floor and shot Lester Beldon in the back."

Dwayne Reddick wrapped a burly arm around Sussman. "Andrew, old pal, remember what I told you the other day about Florida?"

"Florida?"

"Go there, man; you're going bananas."

"Dwayne—"

"Believe me, that's just a crowd noise, Andy. There's fights breaking out around there every night." Reddick smirked. "Hell, it was probably just a pretty girl. Who's that broad with the cement-mixer tits, goes out and kisses people?'' He stacked up his cassettes and put them in a gym bag. "Here you go, Andy, that's everything. Now you send me a postcard from Florida, understand?''

"Right. Thanks, Dwayne.''

"You send me a fruit basket, ship me two dozen of those pink grapefruits—''

"Hey, Reddick,'' interrupted Jack Bryce, "Weaver's going over the match-ups for Boston. Care to join us?''

"Be right there, Jackson.'' Dwayne Reddick turned his tape machine off. "Later, Andy. Enjoy the tapes. Get a nice suntan.''

"Sure,'' said Sussman. Taking the gym bag, he headed away from Reddick's locker and climbed the steps, back into the gym. He grabbed a loose basketball and flung an errant hook shot. Then he buttoned his parka and walked back out into the bright blue February afternoon.

10

It was Monday morning, and Andy Sussman's suspension had now run a full week. He had just finished his grocery shopping and was pulling into the parking lot in back of his apartment building when he noticed a bright red Maserati sitting in his reserved spot. Sussman cursed softly, got out of his car, and stumbled over the frozen slush, wondering whether to call security or just smash the little car into pieces and plow it into the adjoining alley. He examined the Maserati. It was a new model with a patent-leather interior and a sheepskin cover on the steering wheel. There was a small phone connected to the dash and a large radio antenna sticking out of the back, wobbling in the chilly Lake Michigan breeze. The car had no license plates, but had a license-applied-for sticker in the rear window. There was an empty yellow food carton labeled "Egg Roll Emporium" on the passenger seat.

Sussman got back in his car and found another parking space on the street. He picked up his mail, then took the elevator up to his penthouse condominium and slipped his key in the lock. The dead bolt was unlatched. Sussman opened the door and found Murray Glick sitting at his desk, running one of Dwayne Reddick's videotapes through his VCR unit.

"Hoops!" said Murray, shutting the machine off. "I've

been waiting all morning for you, pal. What the hell, I got here at ten, I figured you'd just be rolling out of the sack.''

Sussman set his mail and his groceries on the kitchen counter, pulled off his parka, and shook the snow out of his boots. ''Maserati, Murray? A little showy for a man of your profession, don't you think? What happened to the Firebird, you lose a hubcap?''

Murray pulled the cellophane wrapping off a cigar. ''Firebirds are passé now, Hoops. Strictly middle class. Now this Maz, Hoops, this is the ultimate, I kid you not.''

''Really cuts those turns in the Northbrook Court parking lot, eh, Mur?''

Murray shrugged and searched for an ashtray. ''Hoops, that's what I like about you; you're not impressed by surface glitz. Reality, Andrew, you're my anchor to it, you know that?''

Sussman ignored Murray and pulled a beer out of the refrigerator, breaking an unwritten rule never to consume alcohol before noon on Mondays. ''Murray,'' he said, ''did you know that I pay eight hundred and fifty dollars a month to live in a luxury, *security-proofed* apartment?''

''It's a hot spot, Andrew, I envy you. Lincoln Park! I just love it here in the summer, you can sit right on your balcony and watch the girls walk by—''

''Murray, what I was referring to was the relative ease with which you seem to have broken into my homestead.''

Murray shrugged. ''Gee, Hoops, it was nothing. Not that I've done much breaking and entering lately, but once you get the hang of it, you never seem to lose it, you know?''

''Glad to see you haven't lost your touch.'' Sussman turned his attention to the mail and tore open the top envelope. The return address was CBS Sports in New York, but there was a line through the CBS and the initials DB penciled over it.

"Andy," the letter began. It was written in red ink on CBS Sports stationery. Sussman read it to himself, then out loud for Murray's benefit:

I picked up the *Post* today and what do I find but Andy Sussman, Voice of the Chicago Flames, grounded temporarily for matters relating to the death of fat old Lester Beldon. I tried calling you at CGO yesterday, but no one knows where you are; I call you at your apartment, I get your answering machine . . .

Andy, in case you didn't know it, I'm pushing for you here. We got expanded playoff coverage this year, we got college hoops coming out the wazoo. I got you in the ready file, boy, and now you're mixed up in a murder? Lester Beldon, of all people!

Well I know you didn't do it, Andy, but get things cleared up as fast as you can, savvy? Come regional time in March we've got eight college games in one weekend, so I may be able to do something for you.

You hear??!!

Best,
Danny B.

Sussman placed the letter back on the counter. "Paying attention, Murray? We're talking major breakthrough here, quantum career leap."

"Danny Borenstein," said Glick, walking over to the kitchen and helping himself to some graham crackers and a Pepsi. "How in the world did he ever get so high up there? What is he, a director?"

"Production manager. I think somebody at Wisconsin knew someone in New York, got him started there. He spent two years pouring coffee for Brent Musburger, now he's a big shot." Sussman popped the top off his can of

Pabst. "Murray," he said, "level with me: are we getting anywhere with this case?"

"Of course we're getting somewhere, Hoops." Murray plunked some ice cubes into a glass and poured his Pepsi, which overflowed onto the counter, forming little carbonated puddles on the rest of Sussman's mail. "What we need now are a few theories that might help us find out about the man in the ski jacket, what his relationship to Lester Beldon was, maybe help us figure out who pulled the trigger."

"Fine," Sussman said. "Theorize."

"Okay. First of all, let's talk about motive. Why would anyone want to kill Lester Beldon? He was an annoying, obnoxious bastard, I'll admit, but that's no reason for anyone to blow him away. Is it?"

Sussman shook his head no.

"Now in my experience, honed over six years of practice and a criminology degree at one of the finest institutions in the Midwest, I've found two factors which tend to predominate in matters such as this." Murray began a new sheet on his legal pad; he clicked his pen open and looked up at Sussman. "One: money."

"Profound, Murray. Was that from your master's degree or six years of hardened practice?"

Glick gave Sussman a hurt look.

"Okay, all right. . . ." Sussman took a sip of beer. "Money. Lester was a cheap bastard, Mur. Everything he owned, he got a deal on. His car was a loaner from Covington Olds. All his meals at restaurants he got free, in return for a plug. He had a small house in Wilmette, I was over there once—"

"Did you check his financial records? What did he leave when he died? And to whom? What was his insurance?"

"Murray, how am I supposed to find out all that? You're the detective. Hell, all that stuff I've been reading about eleven-year-olds breaking into NATO computers; you've got a computer—break into the Chicago PD. Break into the Northern Trust—"

"Whoa there, Andrew, breaking into computer systems? That's against the law, pal. They could take away my license." Murray crunched a graham cracker. "Six years, right down the dumper." He sipped his Pepsi. "However, Lester Beldon was a suburban animal. Banks, insurance, investments, I suppose I can check around. Now let's move to page two. Tell me, what do you know about Lester Beldon's women?"

"Women?"

"Yeah. C'mon, Andy, this is the real world. Beldon traveled all over the country, mostly a night here, a night there. He was famous, he was wealthy. He was a fat slob, but most women'll overlook that."

"Murray, Les Beldon was the most loyal husband I've ever seen. I may have thought he was a jerk, but that much I'll give him. Other than all that harmless flirting he used to do, I never saw him sneak a glance at another woman. Every game night, he'd wrap up the show, meet Shirley and take her over to Hathaway's for a drink, then go home. That was it."

"Hoops," Murray said, "did it ever occur to you that if Lester Beldon was having an affair, he might not want to publicize it?" He wrenched a window open and sent a smoke ring floating over Lincoln Park. "Did it ever occur to you that this supposedly virtuous family man, this loving father of five, grandfather of eight, could have been having a sordid affair right under your very nose?"

"No."

"No?" Murray shook Sussman by the shoulders. "No? C'mon, Hoops, use your imagination."

"Even my imagination has limits, Murray. Look, if you think Lester was having an affair, do a little snooping of your own. I certainly can't go up to Shirley Beldon right now and ask her if her husband was seeing another woman."

Murray shivered as a burst of cold air gusted through the open window. "Of course, there's always the drug connection."

"What drug connection?"

"I really think you should get to work on that, Hoops. Have they tested anybody on the team lately?"

"They've got to have some type of reasonable suspicion, Murray, and I can tell you for a fact that they don't."

"What about Lester's autopsy report? Did they find any traces of drugs in his system?"

"I'm sure they didn't find anything stronger than aspirin."

Murray tapped some ashes out the window. "Autopsies aren't done by intuition, Andrew. Get the facts." He looked at his watch. "Speaking of which, it's one-thirty, time to call Susie back."

"Susie?"

"Susie Ettenger. Your attorney, remember? She called while you were out. She said she was going out of the office, but you should call her back at one-thirty sharp."

"Thanks for the message." Sussman reached for the phone that was attached to the kitchen wall.

"Ask her out for dinner while you're at it. She's hot for you, Andrew, I could tell by the tone of her voice."

"Sure, Murray."

"I'm serious. I could feel a definite sense of sexual disappointment when I told her you weren't home. I can tell that in a woman."

"Uh huh." Sussman dialed the number of Susie Ettenger's law office. A receptionist answered and, after a short delay, connected him to Susie. "Susie, hi, it's Andy."

"Oh, hi, Andy," Susie said, in a voice which Sussman

considered devoid of sexual innuendo. "Sorry I didn't catch you before. I got a list from the homicide department today, a breakdown of what they found on Lester Beldon when he died. I'll send you a copy, but I just want to read it to you now, and you can tell me if you hear anything that sounds funny, okay?"

"Fire away," said Sussman, pushing aside Murray, who was leaning on his shoulder.

"Okay, here goes: Lester's wallet, pretty standard—credit cards, picture of wife and children and grandchildren, a grocery receipt, a bank deposit receipt—"

"What bank, Susie? Give me the account number."

"Northern Trust, 342 4387. Also, North Shore Federal Savings, Wilmette Branch, 398 4443. Let's see here . . . Seven wallet-sized, autographed pictures of himself; driver's license; social security; ID cards for American Legion, Kiwanis. Fourteen dollars cash. Gee Andy, he didn't carry much money around."

"He didn't need to, Suse, he never paid for anything."

"All right. . . . Timex watch, Hawaiian shirt, T-shirt, slacks, nothing in pockets—no wait, one ticket to a Flames game."

"One ticket? To what night?"

"February fifteenth. That was the game he was shot at."

"So he had an extra ticket," Sussman said, elbowing Murray. "Somebody didn't show up."

"What are you talking about?" asked Susie.

"Lester gave a bunch of tickets away at Hathaway's Pub a few hours before the game, Susie, but according to this, he held on to one. Obviously he was expecting someone, but whoever it was didn't show." Sussman motioned Murray to make an entry on his legal pad.

"Are you going to make a move with this girl or not?" Murray whispered loudly into Sussman's ear.

"What?" asked Susie.

"Nothing."

"I'll tell Detective Lafferty about the tickets," Susie said. "Now, the overcoat. Are you ready for this, Andy?"

"Yeah, go ahead."

"The overcoat was hanging on the back of Lester Beldon's chair at the time of the murder. It was analyzed by the police department labs because it had a funny odor to it. Turns out, there were traces of gunshot fire, plus some blood. There were also traces of chemicals which were found to be contained in the following substances: Williams Lectric Shave, Vitalis hair cream, Aqua Velva, Old Spice deodorant, Musk lotion, Brut cologne—"

"Sounds like Lester all right. He was probably getting free samples from everyone and felt obligated to use them all."

"Yuck. How'd you sit next to him for three years?"

"It took me about half a season to gauge the ventilation currents in the Stadium. Once I got upwind, it wasn't so bad."

"Small talk," said Murray, "that's good."

"Was that it, Susie?" Sussman asked, elbowing Murray in the stomach.

"I think so. There was nothing else unusual, just a hat, gloves; there was a doctor's appointment card for next Monday—Doctor Montague, a derm in Wilmette. I'll send you copies of everything, okay?"

"Sounds good."

"Ask her out!" Murray whispered, planting an elbow into Sussman's ribs.

"Well, I've got to go," Susie said. "You'll call me if anything else comes up?"

"Er, yeah—"

"Ask her!" said Murray.

"Bye, then."

The line went dead, and Sussman stood holding the phone staring at an incensed Murray. "Pathetic," Glick said, "completely pathetic. I tell you, Hoops, I have use for an attorney now and then, I might give that woman a call myself." He blew out a smoke ring. "I mean, I wouldn't want to move in on you, but if you're not going to do anything . . ."

"Oh sure, Murray." Sussman did not feel threatened. It occurred to him that he might even have a better chance with Susie if she went out with Murray a couple of times first. "Here," he said, presenting Glick with the gym bag full of videotapes. "Do your homework. Take these, too." He handed him the slip of paper with the numbers of Lester's bank accounts on it. "It should be easy for you now. Call me back tomorrow, tell me what you get."

"Fine, fine." Murray grabbed his jacket and headed for the door. "Now why don't you head back to the Stadium, check out those drug rumors."

"Right." Sussman guzzled down the rest of his beer and escorted Murray back to the elevator. "Ciao, Murray."

"So long, Hoops. Be good."

Sussman pushed Murray into the elevator, returned to his apartment, and locked the door. Lying on his couch, he charted alternative courses; chasing down to the Stadium to check out Murray's drug story was hardly the most appealing. More to the point was the matter of Lester Beldon's extra ticket. Who was it left for, and who might know about it? Sussman immediately thought of Charlie Hathaway. Charlie had been at his bar all afternoon—if Beldon had been waiting to meet someone there, Charlie might know.

And what about the crowd reaction Sussman had noticed on Dwayne's videotape? The timing and intensity of the crowd noise still intrigued him. Charlie Hathaway had been at the game, sitting right behind them; he might be aware of a disturbance if reminded of it.

Sussman got up, grabbed his jacket, hat, and a package of Gelusil, just in case he got hungry. It was off to Hathaway's Pub. He had a hunch that if Charlie Hathaway's memory could be jogged, several pieces of the puzzle might fall into place.

11

SUSSMAN REACHED HATHAWAY'S Pub at 2:30, well after the lunch crowd had dissipated, but before the Happy-Hour invasion which had been increasing steadily over the past year and a half. The fact that Hathaway's had weathered the Loop's decade of deterioration at all had always struck Sussman as somewhat short of miraculous. Charlie had often claimed that he would gladly move out to Northbrook or Wheeling if someone would only buy the real estate, but Sussman had a hard time picturing him in those environs; it would have been a migration tantamount to Chief Sitting Bull forsaking Little Big Horn for a condo in Vail. Charlie had somehow held on, and with the regeneration of residential areas surrounding the Loop, he was beginning to get his head above water again. The young professional crowd was beginning to filter in for an occasional drink or light dinner, the athletes were stopping by more often with their autographed pictures, and Charlie Hathaway was even showing occasional signs of enjoying his business.

"Good morning, Charlie," Sussman said pleasantly, finding Hathaway in the little alcove that housed the cash register. He was warding off several waitresses with a stubby right paw while he carried on an animated conversation with Sly Thomas.

84

"Mmmpff," Charlie said, choking on some cigar smoke.

"Morning, Sly," Sussman added, patting the self-acclaimed best-shooting-guard-in-the-NBA on his left arm. "You're out and about awfully early today, aren't you?"

"What you want, Sustman?" snapped Thomas, his face drawn. "You're suspended man, I don't have to give you no interviews."

"We're certainly testy this morning, aren't we? You've got to nurture your relations with the fourth estate, Sly, you might need us when your playing days are over."

"My playing days be going on three more years, at least," Thomas said, looking as aggravated as Sussman had ever seen him. "I got a guaranteed contract, they can't suspend me or nothin'. I'll be outlivin' you in this town, Sustman, that's for sure."

"Andy," said Charlie Hathaway, "give us a couple of minutes, okay? Go sit at the bar and have one on me, I'll be right with you." He turned and shouted to the bartender. "Arnie! Take care of Mr. Sussman, here."

Sussman walked over to the bar, keeping an ear tuned to the conversation at the cash register.

"What'll it be?" the bartender asked.

"Just a Coke, please."

"I want sev'rance pay for her," Sly Thomas was saying, the veins sticking out of his neck. "Two weeks, plus back pay."

"Whaddya mean, severance pay?" steamed Charlie. "She quit, Thomas, she walked out. You don't get severance pay for walking out!"

"What about back pay then? She be workin' here two weeks without a check."

"If she wants her money, she can come back in here and get it. She shoulda stuck around for payday."

"You want some popcorn?" the bartender asked Sussman.

"Nah," Sussman said, trying to catch the conversation at the cash register.

"I oughta dock her two weeks, just for all the trouble she caused me," Charlie was saying.

"Chips?"

Sussman looked at the bartender. Arnie, he thought. Arnie, as in the bartender who had taken Lester Beldon's block of tickets a few hours before the shooting, according to what Charlie had said the last time Sussman was here. "Arnie?"

"Yeah?" The bartender was a tall, greasy-haired kid, about twenty-five, with long, scrawny sideburns and a hint of a mustache. Sussman guessed he was studying nights at Roosevelt College or IIT, or maybe even De Paul. He would probably last one or two years in school, then get a job repairing TVs, or maybe become a plumber. The daytime bartenders at Hathaway's did not seem to exude much of a sense of permanency anymore.

"You were the bartender in here the night Lester Beldon got shot, right?"

"Who wants to know?"

"I do."

Arnie grabbed a packet of potato chips from the wall. "Oh yeah . . . you're the one that got suspended, right?"

"I'm on a brief vacation, let's just say."

"That's too bad. You comin' back soon? I listen to you all the time."

Sussman sipped his Coke. "That all depends, Arnie. Look, Charlie tells me Lester Beldon left some tickets with you a couple of hours before the game, the night he got murdered. Do you remember what you did with them?"

Arnie opened the potato chips and started eating them, the crumbs dangling on his scrawny mustache. "Well, I went, that's for sure. My brother Phil, he went, too. Let's see . . ."

"I heard you had seven tickets. Do you remember what happened to the other five?"

"I dunno. Let's see, there was me, Phil . . . I think maybe Skip Pellios, he went. . . ." Arnie crunched a potato chip. "I dunno, Mr. Sussman. I think I mighta just left a couple on the counter. I do that sometimes; whoever wants 'em takes 'em."

Sussman dug into his pocket and took out the blown-up Xerox from the videotape, with the grainy image of the man in the ski jacket. "You ever seen this guy before, Arnie?"

Arnie took the picture. He held it close to his eyes, then farther away. "Nah," he said, "never seen him."

"Hathaway!" Sly Thomas shouted from the cash register, the rising inflection of his voice catching Sussman's attention. "Hathaway, you just send that cash to Dayton."

"Where in Dayton?" Charlie Hathaway looked at a slip of paper Sly had scrawled something on. "Ain't she got an address?"

"You send it to Bobby, he's gonna be on that Ted Miller thing. That's national TV, right?"

"Beats the hell out of me."

"You just send it to Ted Miller, I bet she gets it."

"Right, Sly. Sure thing." Hathaway relit his cigar and blew a cloud into Thomas's eyes. "I'll send it, but if it comes back, I tear it up, and that's it, understand?"

"Yeah, I understand," Sly said. "I understand you be sendin' a check and that girl be gettin' her money."

"Fine." Hathaway snatched the address from Sly and stuffed it in his pocket. "Now, get the hell out of here, Thomas, you're ruining my business."

"What business, Hathaway? There ain't nobody in here 'cept me an' Sustman, an' Sustman's suspended, he can't even spend no money. Shit, you oughta pay me to be in here, I'd draw you some customers. I come in here for the play-offs, be an expert commentator. Ain't that right, Sustman?'' he shouted across the room.

"You sure won't be playing in any play-offs," Hathaway muttered.

"You take that up with the general manager—I think he stopped workin' the day after he drafted me."

"He's lucky he didn't get fired the day after he drafted you."

"Shee-it." Thomas took a toothpick from a small box by the cash register. "Can't talk no sense to you, man. So long, Sustman," he shouted. "Hope you be back soon."

"Thanks, Sly. You'll be my first interview."

Sly Thomas waved, picked up an empty cigarette pack and hooked it toward a wastebasket. The cigarette pack hit the rim and bounced off, as Sly jogged out the door.

"Same old Sly," sighed Charlie Hathaway, waving Sussman over to a dimly lit table in the back of the room. "All right, Suss, your turn." He tapped his cigar on an ashtray. "Make it short, though. I gotta go home and clean up; I'm taking Irene to the opera tonight."

"The opera?"

"Yeah, yeah, don't gimme any grief. Irene's in this opera club, she goes a couple times a year, I figured it wouldn't hurt to go with her once. Now what is it you want, Andy? You still sniffing after Lester Beldon?"

"Don't get cute, Charlie. They're keeping me off the air until they get this thing cleared up. I've got a future, you know, feelers from the nets. I've got to get my name cleared."

"Tight-assed bastards. You know, I tried to advertise on that station of yours once, Andy, it was a couple of years ago. They wouldn't carry my commercials, not even on the baseball games. They said they're a family station, my place ain't good enough for 'em.'' Hathaway screwed his cigar tighter into the corner of his mouth. "They won't even let the announcers gimme a plug, can you believe that? Goddamn Herbie Blair's been getting free drinks in here for years, he mentions my name once, they bleep it off on the five-second delay.'' Charlie's face was turning red, and his belly rumbled in anger. Sussman always felt uncomfortable when people like Charlie Hathaway got themselves riled up in front of him. What if Charlie busted a vein or had a heart attack, right at the table? Sussman had taken a first-aid course, but he kept confusing CPR with the Heimlich maneuver, and anyway, you'd need a blimp to pump enough air into Charlie Hathaway to keep him alive after a heart attack.

"Take it easy, Charlie," Sussman said. "I'm the one in trouble here.''

Hathaway turned around and waved at Arnie the bartender, who delivered a glass of seltzer water to their table. "All right," he said, sipping the seltzer water as Arnie walked away, "what'd you scrape up now?''

Sussman leaned over the battered wooden table. "Charlie, Lester Beldon had an extra ticket in his pocket when he died. What did he say when he came in that night, do you remember? Was he waiting for anybody?''

"Geez, Andy, I really can't say. We're busy the times he comes in, game nights. Maybe I wave hello, stop at his table, but I can't remember anything he said.''

"Was he with anybody?''

"Ah, you know Lester—he walks over to the bar, glad-hands everyone. Probably tells one of his stupid stories, pats a waitress on the fanny, tells you to watch some guard on Phoenix, turns out the guy was traded to Cleveland two weeks ago. Then he goes to one of the small tables back here and drinks a beer. Come to think about it, Andy, I doubt if he was with anybody. His wife usually comes in with him after the game—maybe the ticket was for her. Shirley went all the time, you know.''

"That's a thought," Sussman said, cradling his soft drink. He'd forgotten all about Shirley Beldon. Lester always had a seat for Shirley across the court from him; she'd be sitting with binoculars, in the VIP seats behind the scorer's table, waving to Lester during time-outs. Sussman decided to check the ticket with Susie and see if it was Shirley's seat. If it was, could there be any coincidence to her being absent the night of the shooting? Could Lester actually have been fooling around? A jealous Shirley Beldon, dyed red hair and J.C. Penney's stretch pants, cooking up a scheme to rub him out? It sounded pretty remote. "Charlie," Sussman said, putting the Shirley Beldon assassination plot aside for the moment, "there's one other thing I want to ask you. I want you to think hard now, okay?"

Charlie Hathaway tapped himself on the forehead. "It's early in the day, Suss. I got no customers and an opera to get to tonight. Try not to make it too depressing, all right?"

"Charlie, I want you to think back to right before Lester got shot that night—the moment before the lights went, can you do that?"

"Okay."

"Now, did you notice anything peculiar, right at that moment? Anything out of the ordinary?"

Charlie screwed the cigar out of his mouth, tapped it in an ashtray and implanted it back between his lips. "Peculiar?"

"Yeah. I've watched the videotape of the game a hundred times, Charlie. Right before the lights went out, just as Sly shot, there was a crowd reaction. A buzz or a cheer, or something. Think hard. Did you hear anything, see anything?''

Charlie shrugged.

"Charlie, how many games have you seen this year?''

"Oh, I don't know, seven or eight. I don't stay to the end, usually. I gotta get back before the rush, and those bums are usually thirty points behind by the end of the third quarter anyway.''

"Charlie, think of all the other games you saw, then think of the night Lester got shot. Try to think if anything happened that night that was different than any of the other nights.''

Charlie Hathaway thought for a moment. He swallowed the rest of his seltzer water, got up, and draped a corpulent arm over Sussman's shoulder. "Andy," he said, "nothing, not a damn thing. Honest, it was just like any other game, aside from the fact that the power went out and Lester got his ass shot off. Maybe you're on the wrong track with this one, kiddo. Call Shirley, find out if she was at the game, maybe you'll get somewhere with her. Now, if you'll excuse me, I've got to go home and take a shower.'' Charlie Hathaway patted Sussman on the back and took a deep draw on his cigar. Then he waddled over to the bar, leaving Sussman sitting by himself in the dark corner.

Nothing unusual, Sussman thought. Everything exactly the same. He drank the rest of his Coke and stared into the bottom of the mug. He had, he mused, seen close to five hundred professional basketball games since he had taken this job three years ago, including exhibitions and play-offs—on the rare occasions when the Flames actually made them. If everything was so normal, so disgustingly the same the night Lester Beldon was killed, then someone, somehow, must have done a helluva good job.

12

ANDY SUSSMAN ENTERED Northbrook Court through the downstairs entrance, wandered into the mall courtyard, and gazed up at the second level. He could see the tall, slightly sloping figure of Murray Glick leaning against the glass counter at Fanny Mae Candies. Murray was talking to a woman with honey-blond hair, who was balancing three plastic shopping bags and a large package against her chest. Sussman could not read the labels on the bags, but they were red and green, with fancy script writing, probably from one of the expensive second-level boutiques. Sussman took the escalator up and sneaked a better look. It was Wendy Altman.

"Hoops!" Murray shouted, spotting Sussman on the escalator, camouflaged by three middle-aged ladies in tennis outfits. "Over here, pal, at Fanny Mae." He waved a bag of candy at Sussman as he made his way over. "Care for a chocolate turtle?"

"That's okay, Mur, I'm on a diet." Sussman tried to make eye contact with Wendy Altman through two bags of shoe boxes. "Hi there, Wendy."

"Hi, Andy," Wendy said, forcing a smile.

"Well, gee," said Murray wedging himself between Wendy and Sussman and looping a long arm around each

one. "Isn't it nice to run into old friends, all at once."
He tapped his heart. "Makes you feel good right here."

"Delightful," smirked Sussman.

"Well, I better not interrupt you two," said Wendy,
tightening her grip on the shopping bags. "I'm sure you've
both got busy schedules. Murray, what time are you picking me up tonight?"

"Seven o'clock, babe."

"Better make it six forty-five. It's hard to find a parking
space by that theater." She turned to Sussman. "We're
seeing David Mamet's new play at the Wisdom Bridge
Theatre. It just opened two nights ago and got great re-
views. It's supposed to be his best since *American Buf-
falo*."

"No kidding," said Sussman. "Sounds like a great
time. Murray, you'll have to tell me all about it at the
game tomorrow night."

Murray smiled sheepishly.

"Don't forget to wear a tie," Wendy said, "in case we
want to go out afterwards."

"Murray, don't you always wear ties when you go to
the theater?"

"Andrew, could we have a word?"

"Bye, fellas," Wendy said, her head disappearing behind the packages.

"Ciao, baby." Murray grabbed Sussman's right arm
and led him into his agency.

Sussman followed Murray into his inner office and
closed the door. "Wendy?" he said, lifting an expensive
cigar from Murray's leather canister. "Wendy *Altman*?
Come on, Mur, surely thou jest."

Glick shrugged. "She walked by the office yesterday
afternoon; I was standing outside, eating an ice-cream
cone, we just got into an idle conversation. Next thing
you know, I'm going to this play."

"You better be careful, Mur, I know how that girl works. She'll start you off with small theaters, then work her way up to the road-show productions at the Shubert. Before you know what hit you, she's talking about what's playing on Broadway, figuring out rates to New York."

"Shared hotel rooms are much cheaper, Andy. I bet she's got a nice body, if you can get past the eight layers of skin cream."

"Yeah, I'd watch it if I were you, pal. You'll have to open up branches in every shopping mall from here to Racine to pay for that girl." Sussman picked up Murray's paperweight with the bullet inside. "You may even have to start dodging these again."

"Nahhh." Murray leaned back in his swivel chair. "I'm in control, Andy, I'm not gonna marry her. If she gets too expensive, I'll dump her—unless she's *that* sensational in the sack, which I aim to find out. Who's this David Mamet, anyway?"

"He's a playwright, Murray, a Chicago boy. Don't try and learn too much about that stuff, though, it's dangerous."

Murray lit a cigar and took a couple of staccato puffs. "Sure," he said. "And while we're on the subject, what about Sweet Susie Ettenger? Did you ask her out to dinner yet?"

"Murray, we have a lawyer-client relationship that I don't think she wants to jeopardize."

Murray shook his head in disgust. "What persistence, Hoops. Honestly, this is just the sorriest romance I've ever been associated with. A girl plays hard to get, you're supposed to go after her; you don't just sit there and wait for her to show up on your doorstep. I'm telling you, Andrew, I might have to ask that girl out myself. I'll end up with all your women, and I'm not taking it off the fee, either."

"What fee? Murray, I thought you were doing this out of the kindness of your heart."

Murray blew a ring of cigar smoke; it drifted up toward the ventilation ducts in the ceiling. "Yeah, sorry about that, Hoops, I guess I am. Speaking of which . . ." He lifted a folder out of his in-basket and spread it on his desk, so that it appeared upside down to Sussman. "This is Lester Beldon's financial data: checking, savings, plastic, plus an account at Vogel and Hempstead Brokerage."

Sussman leaned over the papers. There was nothing remarkable about the checking and savings records; both were relatively low for a man making a six-figure salary, but these days few people left much money in those types of accounts. The Vogel and Hempstead account was slightly more revealing. Lester Beldon had over $50,000 in a cash-fund account, plus $300,000 in various guaranteed securities: T-bills, municipal bonds, CDs, and a thousand shares each in General Motors, Mobil Oil, and AT&T.

"The man sure didn't take any risks," Murray said. "I checked his bank account and canceled checks: no large amounts written to anyone, no large cash withdrawals. I can't see anything shady there."

"What about life-insurance policies?"

"I checked those out, too. Just about what you'd expect, Andy. Three major policies. Half of everything goes to his wife, the rest is split between the kids and the grandchildren."

"Any recent clauses? Any changes that might favor one relative over another?"

"Nothing, Hoops. Dead end. I'm beginning to think we should go back to where we started, try and figure out how the murder was committed, see who was on the scene. Maybe if we can solidify a method and a few faces, the motive'll become more obvious." Murray got up from his chair and walked over to his videotape machine. "I've been studying these tapes, Hoops. I've gone through about twenty-five games—that takes us almost back to Thanksgiving. Now I want you to watch one of these interviews; look at it closely, see if you pick up anything."

The television monitor flashed on, showing Lester Beldon beginning one of his pretaped halftime interviews. Beldon was standing on the out-of-bounds line, about five feet in front of the broadcast table. His leopard-skin card chair was barely visible at the edge of the picture. He was wearing corduroy pants, a light blue shirt with a striped tie and a brown corduroy jacket, which did not quite match the slacks. "Hello again, everybody," Beldon said, "we're at halftime of tonight's game between the Flames and the Boston Celtics, and I thought we'd do something a little different tonight—we're going to talk to that Stadium favorite, the mascot of the Flames, none other than Señor Flame himself! Hey, Señor! Come on over here, fella."

Señor Flame wandered into the picture, his Flame costume pulled completely over his head.

"Now, Señor, being a mascot for a professional team isn't something that everybody aspires to, of course. Tell me, how did you get into this end of the business? Did you ever play the game yourself, were you always a big fan?"

There followed a series of muffled mumblings, which sounded like a Spanish fly caught in a vacuum-cleaner bag.

"Now wait a second, Señor," said Lester Beldon, "I think we might just have to unzip that uniform a little, so we can hear you. For that matter, I'm sure all the Flames fans would like to see that handsome face of yours." Beldon fumbled with the zipper, pulling it down to Señor Flame's navel before the Señor stopped him.

"Careful, Lester," Señor Flame cautioned, holding his hands over his waist. "This is a family show, right?"

"Well, actually, we're on the cable tonight, heh, heh, heh. . . . Just kidding folks. . . ."

As the camera zoomed in on Señor Flame's wan, mustachioed face, Murray froze the frame. "Okay, Hoops, you see that?"

"What?"

Murray pointed to the top right-hand portion of the screen. "That, Hoopsie."

Sussman squinted at the grainy corner, which showed the edge of the broadcasting table in the background. "What are you talking about, Murray?"

"See the chair, Andy?"

"Yeah. . . ."

"What do you see on that chair?"

Sussman squinted again. "I don't see anything, Murray."

"That's right, Hoops. Now. . . ." Murray ran the tape backward about two seconds. "Now, what do you see?"

"I see Lester's coat."

"That's right. Lester's coat is hanging on the chair at Point A, but gone at Point B."

Sussman yawned. "So? Maybe it fell off."

"You think so?" Murray ran the tape forward, slightly past the spot where he had stopped it before. "All right, Hoops, what do you see now?"

"I see the coat back on the chair, Murray. Someone must have picked it up."

"Maybe," Murray said. "But I've run through twenty-five of these tapes so far, and this is the seventh time I've seen that coat disappear and come back. It could be something."

"Murray," Sussman said, "Lester Beldon was a slob. Whenever he showed up, he just tossed the coat on the back of the chair. It could easily have slipped six or seven times over twenty-five games, or six or seven times in one game. Hell, I could've picked the thing up off the floor a dozen times myself, except that it smelled so bad, I didn't want to get near it.''

"Andrew," Murray said, "do me a favor. Do you think you could get that coat for me from the police?"

"Me? Come on, Murray, I'd have to go to the detective station for that. You know I don't want to deal with those guys. Why don't you get it yourself?"

"You're entitled to see the evidence, Hoops. Call your attorney. Let Susie deal with Lafferty; it gives you another excuse to call her, right?"

"I suppose. . . .''

"You suppose? Andrew, do we have to go through this all over again?"

"Murray, can we get off the subject of my love life for just a few minutes?"

Murray took a long draw on his cigar. "Fine, fine. I can only try." He pulled out a legal pad. "Now, Hoops, what about Lester Beldon's wife? Did you get any information on her?"

"Did *I* get any information? I thought you—" Sussman halted his protest, deciding instead to tell Murray about Charlie Hathaway's theory regarding Lester's extra ticket and Shirley Beldon's connection to it. "Now, Murray, here's the thing," he said, after a brief summary of the conversation. "Susie got me the seat number on that ticket—or her secretary did, anyway. I checked it out with the Stadium ticket chart. It was Shirley's seat, just like Charlie guessed. Center court, right behind the press benches."

"So?"

"So? That means Shirley Beldon was supposed to go to the game that night, but for some reason she didn't. Don't you suppose there might be some connection with that and the fact that Lester got killed?''

Murray tapped his cigar in the ashtray. "Hmm . . . well, it's a thought."

"Gee, thanks, Mur."

"The question is, what does it mean? Did Shirley Beldon get the flu, was the whole thing just a coincidence? You were convinced those two were a solid couple, Andy, and we don't have anything to the contrary. On the other hand, Shirley did get half the insurance. Maybe she had some secret lover; maybe she's going to cool it for a while—she's already got the money, right? I think you're going to have to watch her very carefully for a few weeks, see who's hanging around her pantry."

"Murray, get serious—I can't stand outside Shirley Beldon's kitchen window for three weeks, waiting for her to elope with some mysterious stranger." Sussman walked behind Murray's desk and held up Glick's criminology degree from Wisconsin, which was framed and hanging on the wall. Next to it was a certificate from the North-brook Court Vendors Association and below, on the desk, a book of discount coupons from all over the mall. "Murray, isn't this the type of thing that PIs are supposed to do? I mean, I don't mind doing the legwork, but tracking down wayward wives—isn't that right up your alley?"

"*Was* up my alley. I'm into more tangible business now, as you've no doubt noticed." Murray grabbed the coupon book and stuffed it into a desk drawer. "I'll tell you what, Andy, you pay a call on Shirley Beldon, okay? Purely social. You missed the funeral, right?"

"Yeah . . ."

"So you're really sorry, the police were accusing you, you didn't want to upset her. Now you just want to express your concern. Meanwhile, you're over at her house, you nose around; maybe look for a loose phone bill, see who else is with her. Get the idea?''

"Yeah, sure, Murray."

"Good. Come unannounced, though. Don't give her a chance to put anything away. Try and make it around two o'clock, tomorrow afternoon."

"Any special reason for that?"

"Of course. See, Andrew, the way I figure it, by two o'clock things have pretty much begun to accumulate in Shirley Beldon's domicile. The mail's still lying around, phone messages are written out. If you wait 'til four, though, she'll have started cleaning up for dinner, putting things away. That's where experience comes in. Trust me, Andy. Besides, you'll miss the rush hour."

"Thanks, Mur." Sussman reached into Murray's cigar canister, grabbed three cigars for himself, and stuffed them into his coat pocket.

"Hey! Those are expensive, Hoops. I had those flown in from Panama."

"They're terrific, Murray." Sussman tapped his heart. "It's so nice to share things with your friends, isn't it? Makes you feel good right here?"

"Of course, Hoops, help yourself."

Sussman grabbed three more cigars and headed for the door. "All right, Murray. I'll talk to Susie about the coat, then make a condolence call on Shirley Beldon. Meanwhile, you—"

"I'll be poring over the tapes, Andrew. I'm telling you, kid, we're hot on the trail."

"Right," Sussman said. He unwrapped one of Murray's cigars, bit off the end, and lit it with Glick's cigar lighter. He took a few quick puffs, then waved the cigar at Murray and headed back into the mall.

13

SHIRLEY BELDON HAD always struck Sussman as one of those perpetually ingratiating persons, the kind you expected to see at community square dances or ice-cream socials, making sure everyone got enough to eat and no one was left standing in a corner. Recent evidence, however, suggested that this image might have to be altered. What type of tawdry affairs was Shirley engaging in behind poor dead Lester's back? Would Sussman pull up to her driveway and find it occupied by Ferraris and Jaguars, disco music thumping from the upstairs windows? Were there wild orgies going on inside, Shirley snorting cocaine with some Gold Coast commodities dealer, Rod Stewart serenading them in the background ("Do Ya Think I'm Sexy?")?

Or maybe it was something more sedate. Perhaps an insurance man from Des Plaines dropping by when Lester was off in Detroit or Cleveland (Shirley rarely went on road trips). A woman can get lonely, after all. Maybe a chance meeting, waiting for the Linden Street el. A cup of coffee, a slice of cheesecake—suddenly, a revelation: life without Lester could be . . . not so bad! So, Sussman thought, Shirley gets together with her new beau and says, Listen, I've got this great idea. I'll call Lester one night and tell him I'm sick. Then I'll get a gun and sneak underneath the Stadium, short-circuit the power transformer, come back up, and grease the old man. We'll split the insurance, run off to Sun City, and live happily ever after.

Right, Sussman thought, as he pulled up to the Beldon residence, a modest two-storied home in Wilmette, several blocks inshore from the posh Sheridan Road mansions. He stepped over the slushy front walk, rang the doorbell, and listened as footsteps approached from the kitchen. A moment later he heard the sound of locks being unlocked, bolts being unbolted, and chains being unchained. The door opened slightly, revealing a set of curlers; then it opened up a little more to the sight of Shirley Beldon, a *TV Guide* in one hand, a glass of buttermilk in the other.

"Andy?" Shirley Beldon said hesitantly. She was dressed in pale pink slacks, which bulged around the midriff, a navy-blue turtleneck, and a light-green warm-up sweatshirt. "Well . . . Andy Sussman, this is certainly a surprise."

"Shirley, I'm awfully sorry to come barging in like this," Sussman said, wedging a foot inside the door. He was not expecting Shirley to roll out the red carpet for him—although he had sent her a condolence telegram the day after the murder, he hadn't spoken to her at all since then. "I thought about coming by the last week or two, but I didn't want to make things any worse for you, circumstances being what they were. . . ."

"Yes, Andy, I know it would have been difficult." Shirley opened the door all the way. "Would you like to come in?"

Sussman took a quick peek in all directions as he stepped into the front hallway. The dining room and kitchen were to his right, the living room to his left. Straight ahead was the stairway which led to the second-floor bedrooms. Sussman looked for any extra dishes or possessions that might signal the presence of another person, listened for telltale sounds on the floor above him. All he heard was a television set, droning from the kitchen.

"I understand you've been having a rough time, yourself," said Shirley, leading Sussman into the living room. She motioned for him to sit down in an overstuffed easy chair that was cater-corner from the couch. "And I want you to know that I don't believe you had anything to do with Lester's . . . death." She coughed and sat down on the couch. "I hate to say murder, although that seems to be what it is, isn't it?"

"I'm afraid so, Shirley."

"Of course, I know you and Lester weren't exactly the best of friends, and I must admit that some of the things you said from time to time struck me as a tad insensitive."

"I know, I know . . ." Sussman was beginning to feel guilty for the first time since he had discovered Lester dead in the chair next to him. "Honestly, Shirley, I never envisioned a situation like this. You have to understand, sometimes when you work in close contact with someone day after day—"

"Understand?" Shirley gulped down the remainder of her buttermilk. "I was married to him for thirty-seven years, Andy. Every story he bored you with, I had to suffer through a thousand times over. All those locker-room Annies that followed him around, all those fat cigars and smoky joints he dragged me off to . . . I'd just like to know what it was he did that was so terrible, it made somebody *else* haul off and shoot him."

"I'm a little interested myself."

"So I've been hearing." Shirley rose from the couch. "And I suppose I shouldn't forget how to be a good hostess. Can I get you something to drink? I just squeezed some orange juice this morning. Nobody drinks it but me."

"Sure," Sussman said, starting to get up.

"Wait there, I'll be right back," Shirley said. She returned a few moments later with a small glass of freshly squeezed orange juice. "Here you are, Andy. Maybe we should go into the dining room, so we don't spill anything."

Sussman took the glass and accompanied Shirley back through the hallway, stopping briefly to look at the small desk with several letters strewn across it that sat by the front door. The letters appeared to be mostly bills, plus some belated condolence cards and an envelope with the WCGO letterhead on it.

"I've got some sweet rolls in the refrigerator," Shirley said, pulling aside a dining-room chair for Sussman. "I can heat them up if you'd like."

"No, that's okay. . . ." Sussman sipped the orange juice. "I appreciate this, Shirley, and I really would have come earlier, but with all those accusations floating around—I mean, nobody said anything publicly, but I'd just been suspended, and I wasn't sure my coming to the funeral would have helped anything."

"Of course not," Shirley said, patting Sussman on the wrist.

"I just wanted you to know how sorry I felt."

"I'm sure you felt badly, Andy, and I know you had nothing to do with any of this. To tell you the truth, I miss you on the game broadcasts."

Sussman sat up straight. "You still listen, Shirley?"

"Of course I do. You get in the habit after all these years, you know. I heard your voice on the radio so many times. . . . I enjoyed the rhythm of the game, the patter, even if I never paid any attention to who was winning. And after Lester died, and after the first night or two when everybody stopped coming by, I sort of tried to get back into the routine. I'll tell you one thing, Andy, that Paul Wendell, the one that replaced you? He has *no* idea what's going on. Even Lester could do better than him. Do you think they'll let you back soon?''

"Well, I'm hoping so." Sussman took a glance at the mail desk in the front foyer. "Say, Shirley, now that I think of it, that orange juice made me a little hungry—I might be able to go for that sweet roll after all."

"You sit tight then, I'll go back and heat it up."

Shirley returned to the kitchen and Sussman walked back to the foyer, where he quickly rifled through the day's mail. The envelope from WCGO contained a check for $2,593.43, the amount owed Lester up to the time of his death—the exact moment, as it turned out. The accompanying letter from Wilfred P. Brandt apologized for the seeming insensitivity—it was noted on the check that Lester's employment at WCGO had expired, as had Lester, at 9:28 P.M. on February 15—but certain procedures had to be adhered to, and Shirley had, as always, the best wishes of the entire WCGO family. Shirley's first pension check, Brandt added, would be forthcoming. Sussman put the letter back in the envelope. He had not thought about a WCGO pension; he wondered how much it was. He thumbed through the rest of the letters, all bills and junk mail, and returned to the dining room just as Shirley Beldon emerged from the kitchen with his sweet roll.

"I may have burned the cherries a little," Shirley said, scraping away a blackened edge. "I never could get used to that microwave. Lester got it as a door prize at the Christmas party last year and I sort of feel obligated to use it."

"It looks delicious, Shirley." Sussman took a bite of the charred roll. He was trying to lead the conversation to the matter of the extra ticket in Lester's pocket, but wanted to do so without inviting suspicion. "You know, Shirley," he said, "I was thinking back to that night when Lester died. He was in such a good mood, wasn't he? I've never seen someone who seemed so content with the way things were going.''

"I really wouldn't know," Shirley said. "I wasn't there that night."

"You weren't? Gee, I thought I saw you sitting across from us in your regular seat, just like always."

"No, no, I was over at Ellie Rogers's house next door, listening to you on the radio. I was going to go—you know, take the train downtown, then a cab to the game, just like always—but Lester called me up about five o'clock and told me to stay home."

Sussman raised his eyebrows.

"He told me he was going out for a drink with one of the sponsors after the game. He said they had some business to discuss and he'd be home late, so I just stayed here."

Sussman rubbed his forehead. "That sounds sort of funny, doesn't it? I mean, of all the nights to tell you to stay home."

"That's what I thought. And if he'd have gone out somewhere afterwards and gotten shot I'd have been pretty suspicious, but it happened right there at the game, Andy. I honestly can't think of any connection."

Of course not, Sussman thought. There couldn't be any connection, unless dear old Shirley was making up the whole thing; unless she really *was* at the Stadium that night, hot-wiring the electrical circuits, getting ready to blow away her husband. There were ways of checking Shirley's story, of course. He could ask her which sponsor Lester was supposed to have gone out with, but that would arouse too much suspicion—a few strategically placed phone calls could clear that up, and he could check with her neighbor, too. "I can't think of any connection, either," Sussman said to her. "You told the police, of course?"

"Oh, yes. Yes, they got the whole thing, every detail." Shirley glanced at her watch. "I don't mean to rush you, Andy, but I've got some cleaning up to do, and I'm supposed to have dinner with some friends tonight. . . ."

"That's no problem, Shirley." Sussman got up to leave.

"Andy . . ." Shirley stopped and stared at the floor.

"What, Shirley?"

"Could I show you one thing before you go?"

"Sure."

"Come here." Shirley led Sussman out of the dining room, and down into their basement, which had been turned into a paneled rec room, filled with the memorabilia of Lester Beldon's career. There were game programs and trophies and autographed pictures all over the wall. Most of the pictures were from Lester's later years as a broadcaster, all of them showing Lester with his arm around someone, beaming his sappy smile at the camera. Lester and Wilt Chamberlain. Lester in Vegas, with Don Rickles. ("We used to sit right up front, so Don could make fun of him," Shirley said.) Lester with Hubert Humphrey. Lester at a nightclub with a young man in a tuxedo and an older man behind him: "Thanks for your help, Lester, Bobby F." ("Rick Fiorello's kid," Shirley explained. "That's Rick behind him. He played guard on the old Cincinnati Royals. His kid's a comedian—Lester helped him get a booking at Punchinello's.")

"Very nice," said Sussman.

"This is the one I wanted to show you, Andy." Shirley pointed to an eight-by-ten color glossy, taken at the All-Star game that had been played in Chicago two years ago. It showed Lester and Andy standing in front of their broadcast table, their arms around each other. Sussman was trying to force a smile and avoid being strangled by Lester's huge right arm, which reeked of his oppressive combination of colognes and deodorants. Lester was smiling, of course—his huge, gleaming, idiotic smile. The picture was the only one on the wall that wasn't autographed. "Andy," Shirley said, "I know this may sound corny, but it always hurt Lester that he couldn't get you to sign that picture. You know, despite everything, he really had an affection for you. He thought you were the best play-by-play man he ever worked with, and he worked with quite a few of them."

Sussman was beginning to turn red. "Uh, yeah, I guess he did. . . ."

"I know maybe it all seems too late and everything, but what you see here, Andy, this is what I have left of Lester. Now that he's gone, I'd just like to think that he left everything . . . square with everybody, you know?" A tear rolled down Shirley Beldon's face.

"Of course, Shirley." Sussman felt some unwanted salt water accumulating in his own eyes. One of us is an extremely rotten cad, he thought, and I hope it isn't me.

"If you could just think of something to write, Andy." Shirley handed Sussman an orange felt-tipped pen.

"No problem, Shirley." Sussman patted her on the back and uncapped the pen. "To Shirley and Lester," he wrote on the picture, "the real Home Team. All my love, Andy." He clicked the cap back on the pen and returned it to Shirley.

"Thank you," she said, sniffling. "I'll always remember that."

"Glad to help out, Shirley."

Shirley Beldon kissed Sussman on the cheek. "You're so sweet, Andy."

"Anybody would have done the same for Lester."

"Of course." Shirley wiped her tears, took Sussman by the arm, and led him back up the stairs to the front door. "Thanks so much."

"It was nothing."

"I know." Shirley gently pushed Sussman out the door. "Now, if you'll excuse me, Andy, I have to finish doing my hair."

"Right. Good-bye Shirl—" Sussman would have completed the sentence, but he was not in the habit of speaking to slammed doors. He stood on the doorstep for a moment, listening to the lock being locked, the bolt being bolted, and the chain being chained. Then he slogged back through the snow and the slush, into the street, and back to his car.

14

Dear Mr. Sussman:

After due consideration, management has determined that further suspension without pay would constitute an unnecessary and unfair burden on you. Please find enclosed a check for $1,498.26, constituting your salary, minus withholding and other taxes, retroactive to the date of your suspension.

Unfortunately, due to the continuing inconclusiveness of the investigation in re the death of Lester Beldon, I am afraid we must continue to use alternate on-the-air talent during Flames broadcasts. You will continue to receive your salary, of course, and WCGO Radio, on the instructions of our attorneys, will refrain from making any public statements regarding any involvement you may have had with the death of Mr. Beldon.

It is our sincere hope that these actions satisfy the claims you have lodged through your legal counsel. We still consider you part of the family here at WCGO, Andy, and hope that everything is resolved soon and to our mutual satisfaction.

A copy of this letter has been sent to your attorney.

Sincerely,

Wilfred P. Brandt
Station Manager,
WCGO Radio

" 'MUTUAL SATISFACTION . . . PART of the family,' "
Sussman grumbled, as he dropped the letter on Susie Ettenger's desk. "What a crock! They'll leave me twisting
in the wind for weeks."

"Andy, we filed another lawsuit against WCGO this
morning," Susie said. They were inside her eighth-floor
law office at Chavous and Birnbaum—a small windowless
cubicle in the middle of the back wall. "We asked them
to restore you immediately to your full broadcasting du-
ties. We pointed out damage to career and reputation, we
asked for damages of a million dollars—not that we'll ever
get it, but it's a nice round number, and we just wanted
to expedite things."

"How long do you think that'll take?"

Susie shrugged. "It'll be at least a couple of weeks.
These things take time, Andy, and they're probably going
to keep you in limbo for as long as they can."

"Susie, look, I don't have weeks, and I have better
things to do than sit around playing footsie with Wilfre'
P. Brandt. CBS is telecasting a barrelful of college baske -
ball games next month, and Danny Borenstein's trying to
get me a slot in one, but he can't if I'm still under suspicion here."

"Well, you might just have to wait a season, Andy.
Anyway, that'll just add to the damages, and we *will* settle
for something, I guarantee you."

"Oh, terrific." Sussman looked around Susie's work
space, which had a Spartan decor to it. Behind her desk
hung her law degree from Northwestern and her under-
graduate degree from Denison University. There were a
few photographs of family—no boyfriends, Sussman was
happy to see—and a New England sampler hanging next
to the diploma. There were law books spread over the
desk, legal briefs, a bunch of pink memo slips taped to

her telephone. "Okay, Susie," he said, "let's try another tack. I need a small favor from you."

Susie raised a thinly mascara'd eyebrow. "A favor? I'm awfully busy, Andy—I really shouldn't even be talking with you now."

"I know, I know." Sussman gazed into Susie's eyes. The situation had not really called for a personal appearance, but he hadn't seen her in a week, and the telephone seemed so distant. "This is strictly business. I need you to get me Lester Beldon's overcoat."

Susie swiveled her chair around and pulled a file from one of her cabinets. "The one he was shot in?"

"It was on the chair behind him. The police have it, but I think we have a right to inspect the evidence."

"Andy, what in the world do you want with Lester Beldon's overcoat? I thought you were going to stop snooping around."

"I wasn't snooping around. I just happened to be going over some videotapes of Lester's interviews, and I noticed something suspicious."

"About an overcoat?"

Sussman put the notebook down. "Susie, look. You're supposed to be representing me, right?"

"Right."

"And part of that representation is, in addition to proving that I didn't do it, showing that someone else did."

"I'm not a private detective, Andy. It's not my job to pin the murder on someone else."

"But if the evidence is there, you've got to present it. If someone else did it, then obviously I didn't."

"Andy, no one has gotten anywhere with the investigation, I can personally attest to that. I've been checking with the police department every day; they say they don't have the slightest idea who did it, and neither does anyone else."

"I do."

"You?" Susie leaned over her desk toward Sussman. "Andy, you know who killed Lester Beldon?"

"Well, I have a slight idea," Sussman lied.

"Uh huh. Let's hear it."

Sussman began a rambling explanation, detailing his suspicions of Shirley Beldon and her mysterious absence from the fatal game, describing the grainy photo and the mysterious man in the ski jacket.

"You've been doing all this spook work yourself, Andy?"

"Well, you know, I've got time on my hands."

"You went through all those videotapes, from the whole season, and you sat there looking for a little smudge on the side of the picture in a couple of isolated frames? Where did you ever come off as such a meticulous researcher?"

"Hey, Suse, when you've seen as many games as I have, you get observant, know what I mean?"

"Oh, sure." Susie stood up and glared at Sussman the way his mother had when he had brought home a D in algebra his junior year of high school. "Andy, did you go out and hire one of those sleazebag private detectives to poke around for you?"

"Well, not exactly. . . ."

"What do you mean, 'not exactly'?"

"I guess it depends on what you mean by the word 'sleazebag.' "

"By 'sleazebag,' " Susie said, "I'm referring to cheap, whiskey-breathed ex-cops who hang around fleabag motels looking for extramarital affairs; who keep their offices in dingy buildings under the el tracks, are usually wanted in three different states, and end up getting half their clients shot up if they don't get shot up themselves."

"Well . . . if that's your definition of sleazebag, Susie, I can assure you there's nothing to worry about."

"Uh huh. And I suppose you have another definition?"

Sussman cleared his throat. "There are several different species of sleazebag, Miss Ettenger. What you were describing was the genus *Sleazebagus Urbanis Slummis*. I believe the type of sleazebag I'm dealing with is known as *Sleazebagus Mallia Suburbiana*."

"*Sleazebagus* what?"

"Susie, are you acquainted with Murray Glick?"

Susie slumped back in her seat. "Murray Glick? The Sleuth from Sears?"

"He's not from Sears, he runs his own business."

"The Sam Spade of Northbrook Court?"

"What difference does it make where he works? You didn't want someone with an office under the el tracks, remember?"

"Oh, God, Andy, not Murray Glick. The guy's a complete pig, I met him at a party once—"

"Yeah, I know. You seem to have made quite an impression."

"I'll bet I did. Actually, you confused me when you said 'sleazebag.' I don't think 'sleazebag' really captures Murray Glick's personality at all."

"No?"

"Murray's too slick to be a sleazebag. I think 'slimeball' would be much more appropriate."

Sussman paused, considering the word "slimeball" in silent meditation. "Well, I suppose you could say 'slimeball.' A bright slimeball, though."

"Yeah, right. Andy, do you know what your bright slimeball detective tried to pull on me that night? It was a Christmas party at Sherry Dansworth's town house. How Murray got there, I'll never know. I can't believe he ever dated Sherry—"

"Maybe he was on a case."

"Sure, a case of Jim Beam. He pulls me under a mistletoe, Andy, and he gives me this disgusting kiss, then starts telling me how the mistletoe was actually an old Jewish tradition that was started in Jacob's time, and that when two Jews meet under the mistletoe in a Christian household, it's considered good luck to run away to the nearest bale of hay and consummate the relationship."

"Hmm," said Sussman. "Well, I've heard Sholom Aleichem translated many different ways."

"Right."

"But I take it Murray didn't get a chance to test his theory?"

"Murray's lucky I was filled with Christian charity," Susie said. "Or Christian Brothers, anyway. Otherwise, I'd have given him a fat lip."

Sussman backed away. "Hey, Suse, you're one tough broad. I'd better watch my step."

Susie smiled. "I don't think you have anything to worry about, Andy," she said softly. She referred back to her legal pad. "Now what's all this about Lester Beldon's overcoat?"

"Well," Sussman said, wondering if Susie's comment translated into some form of affection, "Murray was poring through those videotapes—he really is pretty observant, incidentally—and he noticed that a couple of times during Lester's pregame interviews, Lester's coat would disappear in the middle and reappear a few seconds later."

"So? It couldn't have slipped?"

"That's what I said. But Murray seems to think that something fishy was going on. Maybe something being passed in the coat, some type of hanky-panky. I'm not sure Murray's telling me everything he knows."

"Somehow, that doesn't surprise me."

"Maybe he's afraid I'll tip someone off. Murray doesn't take too many risks."

"I suppose we should be thankful for that."

"For himself, I mean. I don't think he's too concerned about me getting my ass shot off."

Susie took Sussman's file, closed it, and put it back in her cabinet. "Well, be careful, then, Andy. Now if that's all you need, I've got a meeting in ten minutes." She pulled out her engagement calendar and checked her watch. "I'll get the coat for you."

"Uh, wait one second," Sussman said.

"Wait what?"

"Well, Susie, it occurred to me . . ." Sussman stopped, sensing a totally botched proposal in the making. Oh, what the hell, he thought, and charged on. "I thought, maybe it might be nice if we could, uh . . . have dinner sometime?"

"Dinner?"

"Yeah. You know . . . like food and wine. Salad. In the evening sometime. It's an old American tradition."

"Let's see, dinner . . . ," Susie said, scratching her head. "I think I remember having dinners before I took this job."

"Right!" said Sussman. "So, uh, how about maybe this weekend?"

Susie touched Sussman lightly on the hand. "Look, Andy, I'll tell you what. I'm just so swamped right now. Why don't we try and get your case solved first, okay?"

"Uh, well, okay," Sussman said, hanging his head.

"It's not a no, Andy. I'm flattered, really. But just maybe wait a week or so. Is that all right?"

"Yeah, sure. Of course."

"No, really, I mean it." Susie stuffed some papers into an attaché case and got up from her chair. "Meanwhile, we'll get together from time to time as the client or attorney deems necessary, to discuss progress of the case, okay?''

"That sounds reasonable.''

"Don't hesitate to call.''

"I won't.''

"Good.'' Susie picked up her attaché case and pointed Sussman to the door. "Andy, I look forward to this case being solved as expeditiously and advantageously as possible.''

"Me too,'' said Sussman. "So long, counselor.''

"Bye, Andy.''

Sussman stuck his letter back in his pocket. He put on his overcoat, waved good-bye to Susie, and floated out the door.

15

"RUTABAGA, RUTABAGA, RUTABAGA . . ."

The words came floating through the bowels of the Stadium in a flat, relentless monotone, snaking through the empty lockers and winding through the deserted weight room.

"Rutabaga, rutabaga, rutabaga . . ."

Sussman poked his head into a row of lockers, looking vainly for the source. He tried the whirlpool, then stuck his head into the trainer's room—both were empty. He looked at the clock above the locker-room door; it was 5:15, more than two hours before game time. The players would start to filter in before too long, doing their stretching, getting taped, looking over game films.

"Rutabaga, rutabaga," continued the chanter, from somewhere behind the maze of lockers. "Rutabaga, rutabaga, rutabaga . . ."

Sussman, who would be enduring the fifth game of his suspension, was slightly peeved; he had wanted to be the first one in the locker room, having decided to re-create the scenario leading up to Lester Beldon's murder. He had planned the reconstruction meticulously and had even succeeded in rooting Murray Glick from his Northbrook Court sanctuary; the two would be meeting an hour before tip-off, underneath the west basket. Sussman walked over to the cramped weight room, looking for the vegetable chanter, but found no one.

"Rutabaga, rutabaga, rutabaga," went the voice.

Suddenly, a piercing guitar chord blasted the air, followed by another noise that sounded like an electrical short circuit, followed by a squeaky, off-key black voice. "My baby lo-o-oves meee!" sang the voice, "but I gots to le-e-eave her here ton-i-ight. . . ."

"Rutabaga, rutabaga," the chanter continued, raising his voice as the music flooded through his serenity. "Rutabaga—"

"I gots to go-o-o-o to New Orleans, I gon' be treated ri-i-i-ight—"

"Rutabaga. Rutabaga. Rutabaga—"

A twisting blues guitar riff, registering about a seven on the Richter scale, blasted through the empty lockers.

"Hey!" shouted the vegetable chanter. There was a slight rustling noise, then a loud *"Ouch!"* as a blond head thudded against the bottom of a bench. "Dammit, Thomas, I thought I told you to keep that noise out of here." Jack Bryce pulled himself from underneath the bench where he had been meditating, and held his head, which was cut slightly above the right eye.

"Rut-a-*baaag*-aa!" sang Sly Thomas, gyrating his hips to the music, which came from a portable radio about the size of a small microwave oven. "Whatsa matter, Bryce, I thought your rutabagas be airin' you right out. You look all tense up now, you be in no condition to guard Mack Stewart tonight. Rut-a-*baaag*-aa!"

Bryce, still dabbing his forehead, took three giant strides toward Sly Thomas. He grabbed the radio, opened the back of it, and shook out the batteries, which tumbled to the floor and rolled underneath the lockers.

"Hey, Bryce, what's the matter with you, dude?" Sly grabbed the radio back with both hands. "You goin' crazy?

You be doin' too many of them chants, man, you turnin' into a witch doctor.''

"Thomas," Bryce said, walking over to the sink, "did it ever occur to you that it's important for some of us to prepare mentally for a game, that a proper relaxation therapy will help us perform better?"

"Well, yas sir, Master Jack." Sly scrounged around the floor for his batteries; one had fallen into a crack in the floor, just beyond his grasp. "What you think, man, you own the place?"

Bryce pulled a lock of curly blond hair away from his eye and washed out the cut. "Thomas, it's only twenty after five, what're you doing here so early, anyway? You've got time to eat two pizzas, pick up a waitress, and still be back by seven-fifteen."

"I thought I'd go through my own relaxation tonight, Bryce—maybe do a little of Sly's black magic, do a few chants, put a voodoo spell on Nate Hedricks." Thomas took a bent hanger and pushed it under the locker. "He be guarding me tonight, right?"

"Jesus Christ, Thomas, San Antonio traded Hedricks two weeks ago."

"No shit." Sly gave up on the battery and stood up. "They traded ol' Nate Hedricks?"

"Happy February, Sly. Enjoy it, there's still three days left."

Andy Sussman, who was sitting an aisle over from Bryce, was about to intervene when he heard the door creak open and another stereo fill the room.

"We got *f-i-i-ire* in our eyes," the stereo blared. "We got *fi-ire,* we got *fi-ire* in our souls. . . ."

"Holy Christ," muttered Bryce.

"All right!" shouted Sly Thomas, clapping his hands. "Señor Flame, my man, let's get *down!"*

Señor Flame approached Bryce's locker, his slight body

dwarfed by the stereo in his right hand. He was carrying a large garment bag in his other hand and the combined weight was bending him over like a marsh reed. "Hey, Sly, how you be, bro?" He turned the volume down slightly as he spotted Jack Bryce. "Hey Jack, how you doin'? What you do to your head, man?"

"It's nothing, Señor, just a scratch," Bryce said, holding his ears.

Señor Flame turned off the music. "Hey, I'm sorry, man. I forgot, you're meditatin', right?"

"What you *doin'*, Flame?" yelled Sly, jabbing the Señor in the forearm. "Fuck him, give us some tunes!" He grabbed for the stereo, but Señor Flame pushed it away.

"Thanks Señor," Bryce said.

"No problem, Jack. I gotta go soak the knee, anyway, get myself loose. I got my big comeback tonight." Señor Flame cut across the locker room, spying Sussman, who was sitting by Dwayne Reddick's locker. "Hey, Andy, what you doin' here, man? You back on the air tonight?"

"How ya be, Señor? No, I'm still suspended."

"Sustman?" Sly Thomas poked his head over Bryce's locker. "Hey, Sustman, man, what you doin', spyin' on us? You lookin' for an exclusive story? 'Dr. Sly's Secrets for Gettin' Ready before Big Games'?"

"Sorry, Sly, I work for a family station."

"Yeah? What I hear, you ain't workin' for no one."

" 'Scuse me," said Señor Flame. He put the stereo down on the bench next to Sussman. "Andy, can you keep an eye on this while I soak my leg?"

"No problem, Señor. The doc still got you on two-a-days?"

"Yeah, Andy, another week. Hey, this is my big comeback tonight, you ready for that? First appearance in five games. I got a new routine an' everything. Remember what I was showing you over at De Paul last weekend?"

"I think so."

Señor Flame started the music again. "We got *f-i-ire* in our eyes," the stereo blared, "we got *f-i-ire*, we got *f-i-i-ire* . . ."

Jack Bryce held his ears again.

"Hang loose, Jack." Señor Flame switched off the tape and turned to Sussman. "I got it all figured out, Andy. I'm gonna come in unannounced, be a big inspiration tonight. The fans, they all think I'm still injured, right? We get a few points behind, I come charging right out. I gotta new costume and everything." Señor Flame hung his garment bag over one of the lockers, then headed for the whirlpool.

"Now," said Jack Bryce, "if you don't mind, I'm going to finish my meditation." He walked back around the lockers and sat, lotuslike, in front of his cubicle. "Rutabaga, rutabaga . . ."

A door slammed from the far end of the locker room and Dwayne Reddick rumbled in, toting his gym bag. "Andrew!" he said, slapping Sussman on the back. He led Sussman over to his locker, leaned over, and checked Sussman's complexion. "I don't see any suntan there. I thought I prescribed two weeks of sunshine until this thing blows over."

"Yeah, you're a great doctor. Why don't you book me into one of those retirement homes in St. Petersburg—that's where I'll be by the time this case gets solved." Sussman watched as Reddick loaded a tape into his VCR. "Who're we looking at?"

"Hawk Robbins—he's my man tonight. Someone says he tips his passes—blinks his left eye before he releases the ball, can you believe that?"

"Sheez, Dwayne, you ought to be a biologist or a doctor or something. I can see the headline: 'Dr. Reddick wins Nobel Prize—finds cure for cancer after discovering that white blood cells blink before going to their left.' "

Reddick turned the cassette on and ran the tape forward. "The sad part is, I'll actually figure out how to stop this guy, and we'll still lose by fifteen points."

"*Sly!*"

Reddick was interrupted by a high-pitched shriek from just outside the locker room.

"Sly," shouted the voice, "you can't hide from me, I know you're down there."

"Christ almighty," said Reddick, "that guy's got a trail of women all the way back to the Loop."

"Sly's not here," shouted a falsely low-pitched voice that sounded suspiciously like Sly Thomas.

"Bull-*shit!* Is that you, Sly?"

"Mister Thomas be out on business right now," Sly said again, trying a more dignified tone. "Please leave your message at the front desk—"

"Sly, you get your ass up here—"

"*Rutabaga, Rutabaga, Rutabaga,*" chanted Jack Bryce, raising his voice to drown out the disturbance.

"*Sly!*" The clatter of high-heeled boots stumbling down the cement stairs reverberated through the locker room. "I know you're down here. Hey—" The woman stopped in front of Reddick's locker and stared at Dwayne, who was stripped to the waist.

"Excuse me, ma'am," Reddick said. "The ladies' locker room is down the hall and to the left."

"Stuff it, Clyde, I've seen belly buttons before. Where's Sly Thomas?"

Sussman stared at the woman. She was the same girl who had been haranguing Thomas at practice a week ago; he recognized the red hair and the ratty ski jacket.

"You might try the training room," Reddick said. "Mr.

123

Thomas goes through extensive pregame therapy every night. He may not wish to be disturbed.''

"Yeah, sure," said the woman. "I bet he's drying out somewhere. They got a drunk tank in this place?''

"There's a sauna around and to your right, ma'am. You might wish to knock before going inside.''

The woman turned around and marched toward the sauna room.

"Sly's sure having trouble shaking that one," Sussman said.

"Yeah, she's been hangin' around for a month. Hope he didn't knock her up or anything.''

"*Sly!*" shrieked the woman.

"Hey!" shouted a muted voice from inside the sauna. "What's goin' on! There's a woman in here.''

"There's gonna be a dead man in there, too, if I don't find Sly.''

"Wait, watch my knee," said the voice. The sauna door squeaked open; Señor Flame hopped out and splashed into the whirlpool.

"That woman's got great pursuit," said Sussman. "I wonder if she can dribble.''

"I think she's gonna dribble Sly," Reddick said.

"What you doin' in here, woman?" Sly shouted, still inside the sauna.

"Holy Jesus," said Señor Flame. He turned on the whirlpool, drowning out the rest of the conversation.

"Another chapter of *The Don Juan of West Madison Street,*" said Sussman. "Where do they all come from?''

"That one used to hang around Hathaway's," said Reddick. "The local estuary for basketball Annies and other wildfowl. She worked there, I think.''

"Oh, really?" Sussman raised his eyebrows. There seemed to be an awful lot of reasons to hang out at Hathaway's these days.

"Excuse me, gentlemen," said a tall, sandy-haired man in a camel's hair blazer. "Hello, Andy, you back to work tonight?"

"Hi, Coach. No, not yet, I'm afraid."

"Well, keep your throat in shape." Ted Weaver pulled up a stool and sat in front of Reddick's locker. He was young for a professional coach, only thirty-seven—he had once had a promising career of his own, but a knee injury had forced him into early retirement. He had started his first year with the Flames brimming with high hopes and enthusiasm but now, after two-thirds of a grueling, loss-filled season, Ted Weaver looked drawn. His forehead was wrinkled, his nose was red from constant rubbing, and his slacks were worn at the knees from his habit of kneeling on the floor during games. "How's the tapes coming, Dwayne?" he asked. "You ready for the Hawk tonight?"

"I'm tryin'," Reddick said. "If you could give me a few minutes here . . ."

Weaver cleared his throat. "Uh, Dwayne," he said, "could you do me a small favor?"

"What's up, Coach?"

Weaver pulled a small medicine bottle out of his pocket. "We need a urine specimen. . . ."

Reddick stopped fiddling with the tape machine. He placed his hands on his hips and glowered at the coach.

"Dwayne, it's not my idea, believe me. Some rookie on Seattle got picked up for cocaine in New York two nights ago. He made this big confession to reporters—you know, all that tripe about drugs being all over the league, common as aspirin."

"I don't see how that relates—"

"The owners are jumpy, that's all. Ed Hunter wants everyone to take urine tests, just to make sure—"

"Ted," said Dwayne Reddick, assuming as much of a barristerial aura as he could muster standing half-naked in front of his basketball locker, "I can tell you without even doing the slightest bit of research that the owners have no right to put us through urine tests, unless they have reasonable suspicions of illegal drug use."

"I know, I know," Weaver said. "Look, Dwayne, legally you can make an issue out of this, but do me a favor. You and I both know you don't use drugs. Management's on my case to do this, I've got enough trouble just trying to get a team out there that won't get embarrassed every night."

The door to the sauna slammed open, and Sly and the red-haired girl stormed out. "You talk to him," the girl said, "you make him hear some sense—"

"Sense, bullshit," said Sly. "I don't see no difference whether he shows up or not."

"Cram it, Thomas," shouted Jack Bryce.

Dwayne Reddick turned his VCR off. "Ted," he said to the coach, "it's not that I'm afraid of anything, you know me, but if you let these guys chip away at your rights, you won't have anything left of your self-respect."

"Dwayne, listen," said Weaver. "Just ask yourself, is this the place to make a stand? We're twenty games in the hole, we got five-thousand boo-birds here every night; do we need our star player refusing to take a drug test?" He wiped his forehead with a soiled handkerchief. "We've only got eighteen games left, Dwayne; do we really need that?"

Reddick grabbed the bottle from Weaver's hand. "Fine, fine . . . Hell, what's another compromise."

"Sly!" shouted the woman, wrestling with Thomas, trying to push him into the whirlpool. "You listen to me; Bobby can't do no benefit—"

"Let go of me, woman."

"Watch out!" said Señor Flame, still soaking his knee in the whirlpool.

"Hey, Ted," Reddick said, inspecting the urine bottle, "how about Sly, there? You going to get a test out of him?"

"We got one yesterday."

Reddick raised his eyebrows. "Funny, I didn't hear any screaming."

"We put a Y-joint in the urinal drain and tapped it out without telling him—"

"You *what?*"

Weaver sighed. "Look, Dwayne, we wouldn't do that to you, believe me."

"Hey, sure, I believe you, man."

"Dwayne, look, what do you want from me?" pleaded Weaver. "Stick up for me, I'll stick up for you." He turned around and headed for Jack Bryce's locker.

"Yeah, you got it, Ted."

"Sustman!" A dripping-wet Sly Thomas staggered over to Sussman, a soggy towel draped around his waist. He was dragging the red-haired woman by the sleeve of her dirty ski jacket, which was oozing slime from the sauna and the whirlpool. "Now we talk some sense, woman."

"We don't talk nothing, Sly—you keep your mouth shut."

"Sustman, you hear about that benefit they're throwin' for ol' dead Lester Beldon next week?"

"Benefit? What benefit?"

"For the Cancer Fund, or whoever it was he made his will out to."

"I don't think anybody told me about that."

"Well, now ol' Sly be tellin' you, man. They want to honor fat Lester's memory, so they're havin' a benefit at Hathaway's the fifteenth, eight o'clock sharp. All Lester's friends buyin' plates for twenty-five dollars, the money all goes to Lester's favorite charity. You be goin' to that, Sustman?"

Sussman shrugged. "Hell, I don't know, Sly, if they ask me, I suppose I'll go."

"See!" Thomas said to the girl. "Sustman's still a suspect in this case, woman; dumb-ass detectives think he did it, an' *he's* goin'. Now you tell ol' Bobby to get his ass over there, honor his godfather or whatever he is— *ouch!*" Sly held his shin, where it had been kicked by the woman's pointed boot. "You be careful, woman, that's my shootin' foot."

"Go soak it in the frigging sauna," said the girl. She kicked Sly in the other shin.

"Arg!" screamed Sly, as the girl stalked out of the locker room.

"Gee, Sly, locker rooms can get to be pretty dangerous places."

"Later, Sustman." Sly grabbed his right shin, then his left foot, then limped back to the whirlpool.

"Well, there you have it," said Dwayne Reddick, sitting in front of his locker, a towel draped over his broad shoulders. "All my life I worked for this. Days, nights, summers, practicing jump shots, pumping iron, going over these damn tapes every day."

"Aw, Dwayne, get off the rag, it's not so bad."

"So I get the honor of being asked to prove I'm not a junkie instead of having the urinal tapped on me."

Sussman gave Dwayne a friendly poke in the ribs. "I thought it was an outstanding show of trust, befitting your status as elder statesman." He looked at his watch. "Got to go, Dwayne, I'm meeting somebody at six-thirty."

"Not that pretty little lawyer you were telling me about, by any chance?"

"No such luck. Just some more casework."

"All right, buddy. Need any more tapes, let me know."

"Thanks, Dwayne. Have a good one tonight."

"Gotcha, Andrew."

Sussman left the lockers and headed up the stairs. His pregame stakeout had not revealed any killers, but trinkets of information were starting to filter down. It was time to see what Murray Glick had come up with.

16

"DRUGS," SAID MURRAY GLICK, with a look of finality. "I've been telling you for two weeks, Hoops, it has to be drugs."

"Oh, come off it, Murray; they're taking one test, and it's only because some guy in Seattle shot off his mouth." Sussman sagged against the basket support at the west end of the Stadium, where he and Murray were watching the San Antonio players go through their warm-up drills. It had always irked him that people associated drugs so freely with this sport and with his friends in it. He couldn't deny that drugs existed around the league—just like they had existed in college and even in high school—but most of the players he knew were clean, and the thought that Lester Beldon could be involved in a drug deal seemed so remote as to be laughable.

"It's not just the guy in Seattle," Murray said. "This *is* pro basketball, Andy—grass, pills, coke. It goes with the territory."

"Sure, Murray, you're exactly right. And all the players make a million dollars a year, and the games are all decided in the last two minutes, except the ones that are fixed."

"I wouldn't know about that, Hoops. I never stayed at

a Flames game past the third quarter. But I am convinced there's drugs involved here; everything points to it.''

"What everything? One theory of yours about a coat being passed back and forth? We've got no solid suspects, our victim had no enemies, if there was anything between him and his wife, I haven't figured it out. . . .''

Murray stretched his elongated frame and leaned against the basket support, watching as a San Antonio player casually jammed a pregame dunker. "Sorry, Hoops, I know you're friendly with these guys, but let's face it—pot, cocaine, it's all over the league, especially on a bunch of losers like the Flames. How do you think they make it through a season when they're twenty and forty-five?'' He craned his neck and peered over the mostly empty stands. "Forty-eight hundred tonight, Andy, five thousand, tops. Not even enough to pay the ushers. I think we might have to leave earlier than usual, maybe mid–third quarter.''

"Murray, why does the size of the crowd dictate when we have to leave the game?''

"Because, Hoops, if your boys are thirty points behind by halftime like they usually are, there'll be no one left here at the end—and I am *not* wandering out onto West Madison Street at ten-thirty at night without the benefit of a crowd.''

Sussman scooped up a loose basketball and tossed it to one of the San Antonio players, then turned back to Glick. "Look Murray, let's get back to basics. I sat in that locker room for an hour and a half, trying to figure out who shows up early, who would have had access to the fuse board without anyone knowing. There's some funny things going on down there, drugs or no drugs.''

"Drugs, Andy. We just have to figure out the whys and the wherefores.''

"Right. Murray, forgive me, but I just have trouble visualizing Lester Beldon as the center of some NBA-style

French connection. Hell, the guy could barely hold down a couple of beers. The strongest drink I ever saw him order was one of those tutti-frutti cocktails at the Christmas party a couple of years ago—you know, one of those pinkish blue jobbies with the little umbrellas, where you get to keep the glass?''

"I didn't say he *used* the drugs, Andrew. Now, let's go over your locker-room scene again. Reddick, I'll take your word for as clean. Weaver, too. Who else was down there?''

"I told you about Jack Bryce, trying to do his meditation.''

"Bryce, the hippie center?''

"He's not a hippie, Murray. The guy's got an economics degree at Berkeley.''

"Uh huh.'' Murray pulled a cigar out of his pocket. "So what do you call a six-foot–ten-inch white guy with curly hair and a college degree who lies under a bench chanting mantras an hour before the game? You don't think that's a candidate for a little controlled-substance action?''

"Sure, Murray, cut and dried. Get a warrant.''

"We'll look into it. Who else?''

"Señor Flame.''

Murray shook his head. "Sorry, the man's got no money. Go on.''

"Well, there's Sly, of course—although they watch him pretty closely. And that girlfriend of his, she's been ragging him for a couple of weeks. She was getting pretty worked up down there.''

"Ah, Andy, that guy's got so many broads after him . . .''

"Yeah, but this one's been persistent. She had a panicky look in her eyes, you should have seen her when Sly came up and asked me if I was going to some memorial dinner they're throwing for Lester next week. Why should either of them care about a memorial for Lester Beldon?''

''Why would Sly come up and ask you about it, if he's got something to hide?''

''Maybe he doesn't, Mur. But why did that girl want to keep him from mentioning it in the first place?''

''I could really use a hot dog,'' Murray said, gazing longingly at the lobby.

''The hot dogs are poison here, Murray—there's enough grease in 'em to keep a tank rolling for a month.''

''One won't kill you, Hoops. We'll get the kosher ones.'' Glick watched as the San Antonio players finished their warm-ups and congregated around their bench. ''Whoa, Hoopsie,'' he said, as a line of scantily dressed women came trotting onto the court. They wore tight-fitting red and orange sweaters with a silver F on the front, and bright yellow miniskirts. ''What have we here?''

''Those are the Flamettes, Murray. They just started last week—another one of our futile gestures to get some fans in here.''

Murray whistled.

''Stop salivating. They've got two extremely large, hairy-chested guards, just in case you get any ideas. Speaking of which, old buddy, you never told me about your date with Wendy Altman.''

Murray flashed a Cheshire Cat grin. ''I didn't? An unwitting omission, I'm sure.''

''Right. Murray, you're stretching my imagination without even saying anything.''

Glick continued grinning and headed away from the court.

''I don't suppose there are any words behind those teeth.''

''Yeh heh heh,'' chortled Murray. He followed the aroma of greasy hot dogs into the lobby.

"Forget it. Forget I even asked."

"It's a great story," Murray said as he arrived at the concession stand.

"I can hardly wait."

"Halftime, Hoops."

"Sure thing."

"I'll give you all the details."

"What'll it be, Mac?" asked the concessions vendor, dipping his fork into a pan of greasy, precooked hot dogs.

"Three kosher hot dogs," said Murray, pulling out his wallet. "Two beers, two peanuts, a Mars Bar, a hamburger, and a salted pretzel." He turned to Sussman. "Game starts in fifteen minutes, Hoops, might as well stock up. Now, what did you want?"

The basketball game was midway through the second quarter, and it was already beginning to take on the pattern of most Flames contests. The Flames had broken in front early, thanks to some uncharacteristically hot shooting from Sly Thomas and the steady play of Dwayne Reddick. After nine or ten minutes, though, their game had started to disintegrate. Bryce, the center, was being worn down by his taller opponent. The San Antonio guards began picking up Sly Thomas farther away from the basket, and Sly cooperated by shooting twenty-five-foot jumpers that ricocheted off the rim. The score was 28–23 in San Antonio's favor by the end of the first quarter, and five minutes into the second quarter the lead had been stretched to thirteen points.

Sussman and Murray were sitting in Murray's seats, which were in the loge section, by the west free-throw line, fifteen rows back. Sussman had brought his transistor radio along and hooked up his earphone. He wasn't sure what disgusted him more—the Flames' play or Paul Wendell.

"Here's Ralph Rogers—make that Jackson—bringing the ball up for San Diego," Wendell was saying. "He passes the ball—no wait, he fakes, he dribbles toward the basket—there's a whistle, that's traveling—no, three seconds—no wait—"

"All right, Murray," Sussman said, pulling the earphone out of his ear, "I can't wait 'til halftime. I want the truth. Did you sleep with Wendy Altman the other night?"

Murray gulped down his second beer. "Hoops, I'm shocked. Do you think I'm the kind of guy who brags about his conquests?"

"You want me to name every girl you've allegedly slept with in the past year?"

"This is just a time-out, Hoops; wait 'til halftime if you want to go over the whole list. Besides, what do you care if I slept with Wendy Altman? You could have had her if you wanted."

"Yeah, right. Your place or hers, Murray?"

"I don't think that she'd even consider coming to my place without a police dog and an inspection team from the sanitation department," Murray admitted.

"So it was her place?"

"Are you kidding? Ever tried to get in her apartment, Andy? She's got so many locks on that door, she looks like she's expecting the Russian army."

The Flames scored on a steal and a lay-up, but Sussman ignored the game and continued his inquisition of Murray. "So where was it, Mur? You didn't do it in your Maserati, did you?"

"Well, you're on the right track." Murray paused to rip open a bag of peanuts. "When I saw she wasn't going to let me in, I turned to Contingency Plan A. I said, 'Hey Wendy, you know what I feel like right now? A nice game of miniature golf.' "

"Miniature golf? In February?"

"That's what she says. So I tell her I know this place out west of Rolling Meadows that has a dome on it for all seasons—you know, one of those Teflon bubbles?"

"The only place I know in Rolling Meadows with a bubble on it is Ed Olmstead's Mercedes place."

"Right," Murray said. "But Wendy's a North Shore girl, she doesn't know from Rolling Meadows. And I solved a case for Ed Olmstead a couple of years ago. He told me if I ever needed a favor to give him a call."

"You planned this whole thing out in advance?"

Murray furrowed his brow in a manner that suggested that the Olmstead maneuver was typical of his preparations for a potentially romantic evening. "So I get to Olmstead Mercedes," he said, "and I say, 'Look at this, Wendy— there *used* to be a miniature golf course here; I wonder what happened—it's a Mercedes place now.' And, of course, I had a key that just happened to fit the showroom door."

"Wendy fell for that?"

"She was pretty impressed when the alarm didn't go off—not to mention the erotic pleasure that only Wendy Altman could get from a brand-new Mercedes-Benz."

A referee's whistle interrupted Murray and shattered the pall that had settled over the sparse crowd. Sussman looked up to see what was happening. One of the officials was signaling a technical foul on Sly Thomas. Sussman plugged in his earphone.

"I think the officials called another time-out," Paul Wendell was saying. "No, wait, they may have called traveling. . . ."

Sussman pulled the earplug out. "Old Sly's pretty hyper tonight," he said, as Sly wrung his hands in the air and continued to jaw at the official. "He usually doesn't pick up his Ts until the third quarter."

"I'd like to see that guy's dope test," Murray said. "Speaking of which, did you get the results from the blood and urine tests on Lester Beldon's autopsy?"

"Susie got 'em, she said they were all negative."

On the court, the San Antonio player made his free throw and the Flames took Sly Thomas out of the game. The crowd booed although Sussman was not sure whether they were booing the referee, Sly, or Coach Weaver for making the substitution. San Antonio now led by seventeen points as they inbounded the ball.

"Also, I was wondering," Murray said, "did you check out that doctor's appointment card they found in Beldon's wallet?"

"That was for a dermatologist."

"That's what it *said*, Hoops. Any doctor can dispense drugs. And besides, you know that nose operation they do for coke heads?"

"Murray, dermatologists don't fix noses."

A loud cheer went up from the crowd.

"What was that?" Sussman turned around and focused his attention back on the game. Dwayne Reddick had grabbed a rebound and was standing in the backcourt holding the ball, waiting for one of the guards to come back and take the pass. Nothing remarkable seemed to have happened. The cheering increased, however, becoming especially loud on the side of the building where Sussman and Murray were sitting. Sussman stood up, trying to see what the commotion was. Suddenly a sound blurted out of the loudspeakers.

"We got *f-i-ire* in our eyes. We got *f-i-ire*, we got *fi-i-i-ire*, in our souls. . . ."

Sussman looked down behind the Flames' bench. Running through the courtside seats, dressed in his brand-new orange-and-blue costume, was Señor Flame.

"We're the *fl-a-ames* of insurrection," played the record, as Señor Flame did his voodoo dance and the crowd cheered. "We're the *s-o-ouls* of resurrection. . . ."

"Holy shit!" said Sussman, slamming Murray on the leg. "Señor Flame! I should have figured that out in a second!"

"Come again?"

"They're cheering for Señor Flame, Murray! Hell, it was staring us right in the face. Remember the videotape of Lester's murder?"

"Andrew, what're you talking about?"

"Right before the lights went out, Murray, while Sly was starting to shoot. The crowd started to cheer, remember?"

Murray crunched a peanut.

"Murray, look, imagine you were at the game that night. The fuse is all set, right? It's ready to blow, the lights are about to go out. Now, just before all that happens, who should suddenly show up at courtside? Think about it; who else could have made the crowd cheer when nothing was happening in the game?"

"Hoops, I'm not sure that goes along with my theory—"

"Just answer the question. Who got the crowd going?"

"Andy—"

"Who slipped behind the broadcast table and stood right behind Lester Beldon—"

"Hoops—"

"—the instant before Lester Beldon got blown away?"

Murray Glick looked at Andy Sussman.

Andy Sussman looked at Murray Glick.

"Señor Flame," they both said.

17

ANDY SUSSMAN STOOD cramped against the pay telephone in a dark, musty corner of the Stadium lobby, the phone cradled under his right ear. "Yeah, Phil," he said into the phone, "February fifteenth, just before the third quarter ended . . . all right, I'll wait. . . ."

"Does it check, Hoops?" asked Murray, who was munching on a hot salted pretzel.

"Phil Mariola's checking his tapes back at KPST in Phoenix. We'll see what he picked up. It figures, though, Mur. Remember what I told you about Charlie Hathaway?"

"I still don't know about this, Hoops."

"He told me he couldn't remember a single unusual thing that night. And Señor Flame was strictly routine, Murray. He had the perfect cover. He comes out every night, he dances, the crowd cheers . . ."

"It just doesn't wash, Andy. There was no reason for the crowd to react that night the way they did just now. Tonight was Señor Flame's big comeback, everyone went crazy."

"Well, maybe it was the first time he'd been out that night. Wasn't that the game he wrenched his knee? Maybe he's down there icing it the whole first half, then, when he makes his grand entrance in the third quarter, the crowd goes wild. Except Señor Flame really didn't hurt his knee—he faked it, so he could stay down in the locker room after halftime. When everybody's back upstairs, he sneaks to the power board and plants his charge; then he stuffs the gun under his costume, comes back, and greases Lester. By the time the dust clears, he's back in the whirl-pool and no one's the wiser."

"Could be," Murray said, unconvinced. "But it goes against every shred of evidence I've got."

"You don't have any shreds of evidence."

"Look, Hoops, I've been going over this drug theory of mine, and Señor Flame just doesn't fit the profile. He doesn't have the money or the lifestyle, he wouldn't have the contacts—"

"Hang on," said Sussman, getting back to the phone. "Yeah, Phil, you got it? . . . Good. . . . No, don't worry about the video; we get the same feed, I've already seen it. Just turn the audio up and let me hear your call." Sussman motioned to Murray. "Okay, Mur, they've got it cued up." He held the phone to his ear and listened to the audio portion of the tape.

". . . A minute-ten left in the third quarter as Chicago brings the ball upcourt, trailing the Suns seventy-eight to sixty-two. Ronny Long takes it over midcourt, looking for Branch. Branch kicks it off to Sly Thomas. The crowd's cheering about something, I don't know what. Thomas is guarded closely by Sam Draper. What's going on down there, Bill? Wait, I get it: it looks like the Chicago mascot just came out—we haven't seen him all night. Now Sly Thomas tosses up a long jumper; I don't think it's got a prayer, it is . . . ." The tape faded to silence, as Sussman envisioned the vapor lights at the Stadium draining into darkness.

"That's it," said Phil Mariola. Sussman could hear him click the tape off over the telephone. "That's all there is."

"That's all I needed," Sussman said. "Thanks, Phil. . . . So long." Sussman hung up the phone.

"So?" said Murray, who had purchased a beer in the meantime.

"It was Señor Flame, all right."

"You're sure? You saw him?"

"Phil Mariola saw him."

"With a smoking gun pointing at Lester Beldon's corpse?"

"Sorry Mur, they didn't have a close-up shot of Señor Flame pulling the trigger. I'll call their director in the morning and see if he can work on anticipating murders a little better."

Murray slurped his beer wordlessly.

"Come on," Sussman said, grabbing Murray by the arm. "Let's go downstairs and see what Señor Flame has to say for himself."

Señor Flame sat bewildered on a bench beside his dressing area, a detached section of lockers that was several feet removed from the players' dressing quarters. "What're you *talkin'* 'bout, Andy?" he said, beads of sweat pouring off his forehead, which was still engulfed by his half-zipped Flame costume. "You think I killed Lester Beldon? Are you crazy, man?" The game had ended fifteen minutes ago. The Flames had lost by twenty-three points, and most of the players were dressing silently or lingering in the showers until the few reporters still covering the team had left. "Andy, you're going nuts! What've I got against Lester Beldon? Why would I want to shoot the guy? Besides, I wasn't even there; I got my knee banged up, I was in the hospital."

"Don't tell me you weren't there, Señor. I just listened to a tape of the Phoenix broadcast. I heard Phil Mariola say he saw you out there."

"Hey Sustman!" Sly Thomas walked behind Sussman and placed a sopping-wet hand on his sport jacket.

"Sly, do you think you could try removing the sweat from your body before you start these displays of affection?"

"That's not sweat, Sustman, that's soap suds. Goddamn shower be shuttin' off in the middle again—hey, Glick!" Sly reached for Murray, who was hiding behind Señor Flame's costume. "What your ass be doin' down here, Glick? Some little girl's daddy after me again? I'm tellin' you, man, I'm clean of that shit."

"Sly, do you think you could give us some privacy for a few minutes?" Sussman said.

"What you think, you own the locker room?" complained Sly. "Hell, you ain't even accredited anymore."

"Sly, go jump in the whirlpool."

" 'Sides, Sustman, I got a favor to ask you."

"What could I possibly do for you, Sly?"

"Just come over here, we gotta talk."

"Later, Sly. Gimme ten minutes, okay?"

Sly blew a soap bubble off his arm. "Sure thing, dude. I be waitin'." He waved and slipped off to the whirlpool.

"All right now, Señor," Sussman said. "Why don't you just tell us what happened that night?"

"How do I know what happened? I'm tellin' you the truth, Andy, I was hurt. I was in the hospital."

"What hospital?"

"Northwestern, man. That was the day I hurt my knee, wrenched it in practice doin' a double whirl. Doc Kellerman put some ice on it, sent me over there to get X rays. They tell me I gotta sprain, gotta stay off it and take more tests, so they keep me overnight. Hell, Andy, I got the records and everything."

"So you were at the hospital the whole night?"

" 'Til two o'clock the next afternoon, Andy. Then they give me crutches and an Ace bandage and say I can leave."

"Excuse me," said Murray. "Señor Flame?"

"Who's this guy?"

"Señor, this is Murray Glick, he's a friend of mine. Murray, this is Señor Flame."

"You givin' him these crazy ideas?" Señor Flame asked, pulling his arms out of his costume. "Hell, I got enough trouble just tryin' to dance. Look, Andy, I gotta go soak this knee."

"We'll let you go in just a second," Murray said, finishing off his beer. "Now Señor, I want you to think back to that night you spent in the hospital, can you do that?"

"Yeah, man." Señor Flame rubbed his knee underneath his costume. "It wasn't bad, actually. I had a semiprivate room, they bring you meals and everything."

"Señor," Murray said, "when they made you stay overnight at the hospital, you had to tell someone on the team, right?"

Señor Flame nodded his head. "Yeah, sure, I hear you. I call up about four, tell 'em to count me out for the game that night."

"Call who up?" Sussman asked.

"I dunno. I musta called the training room to tell Doc."

"At four o'clock?" Sussman said. "Who's down here at four, Señor? Freddie Granger eats dinner early so he can get here by five and start taping guys up. Doc Kellerman doesn't show up until six-thirty."

"Hell, I don't know, Andy." Señor Flame began pulling a brace from his right knee. "I'd just been through three hours of testing, I was upset about missing the game. I just called down here, somebody answers. They said they'd tell Freddie or Doc and hung up. Honestly, Andy, that's all I know. I was hurtin', man."

"Hey, Sustman!" bellowed a voice from the whirlpool. "I be waitin' on you, man."

"You mind if I go put some ice on this thing?" Señor Flame said, pointing to his knee. "We got another game tomorrow night." He put his Flame suit on a hanger and hung it in his locker. "Back-to-back games, just what I need right now."

"Sure, Señor, go ahead." Sussman patted Señor Flame on the back and wandered over to the whirlpool, with Murray trailing behind. "Now, Sly, what did you want?"

"Glick, what you *doin'* here, man?" Sly splashed some water at Sussman. "Get him outta here, Sustman, I don't need no po-lice snoopin' around."

"Sly, baby, I was on your side, remember?" Murray said, wiping whirlpool foam out of his hair.

"Yeah, well I ain't payin' you now, which means you're workin' for someone else, 'less you just came down here to admire my beautiful athletic ass."

"That's too disgusting to even think about," Glick said. He wandered back toward the trainer's room.

"Jus' keep your butt outta here," Sly shouted, then turned back to Sussman. "Is he workin' for you, Sustman?"

"Just giving me some friendly advice."

"Well, I got some friendly advice for you, too. Help you get your career back together again, get your ass back on the air before the season ends."

"Glad to know you're so concerned about my welfare, Sly."

"Now this is just between you and me," said Thomas. He motioned Sussman closer, then cupped his hands and whispered. "I hear there's a TV job opening up in Indi'napolis, 'bout a week. The regular guy, he bein' investigated for shopliftin', lotsa other shit, too. They 'bout ready to run him out of town."

"Pete Turner?" Sussman looked at Sly in disbelief. He only knew Turner from the several times during the season when the two teams met, but he seemed like a fairly stable guy, a down-home Indiana type. "Where'd you hear about this, Sly?"

"Word's getting out, man. R.D. Bridger, used to play ball with me down in Georgia, he givin' me all the facts. You should call, Sustman. The way the po-lice draggin' their ass on this investigation, they never gonna clear things up here."

"Oh, yeah? You've been following the story?"

Sly stepped out of the whirlpool, his lower body covered in foam. "I don't need to follow it, Sustman, I just be followin' you, an' you ain't workin' yet. 'Sides, everybody knows those dudes at 'CGO be lookin' for an excuse to dump you. You take that job down in Indi'napolis, they'll end their investigation real quick. They'll say, 'You're clean now, Sustman, long as you get your ass out of Chicago.' Toss me that towel, will you?"

Sussman tossed Thomas a mangy towel. Sly caught it, wrapped it around his waist, and headed back for the lockers.

"You take my advice, man."

"Yeah, yeah," Sussman said.

"Go to Indi'napolis, start your comeback."

"Andy!" shouted a voice from behind.

"Right here," Sussman said.

"You got a phone call, man."

Sussman turned around and saw Freddie Granger, the trainer. Short and stocky, with slick black hair, Granger was still dressed in the sweat shirt and cotton slacks he wore while sitting on the bench during games.

"Some broad," Granger said.

Sussman walked over and picked up the phone. "Hello?"

145

"Andy?" said the voice on the other end.

"Yeah?"

"It's Susie."

"Oh, hi . . ."

"I'm sorry to call you like this, but you said you were going to go to the game, and I just figured you might be down here. Did you find out anything?"

"Er . . . ," Sussman said, his hand cupped over his mouth.

"That's okay, you can tell me later. Listen, remember that coat you wanted me to check on?"

"Lester's overcoat?"

"Right. I finally got through to the police. They said it's all right if we look at it, but they don't want the evidence to leave their possession."

"So we have to go down there?"

"Right. And normally they'd be closed 'til Monday, but I got the sergeant to agree to let us come in and take a peek, if we get there first thing tomorrow morning."

"What's their definition of first thing?"

"Seven-thirty. Ashland Avenue station."

"Ouch."

"Come on, Andy, you're not even working, what do you care? I was supposed to have Saturday off."

"Well, I suppose I can make it. You mind if I bring Murray along?"

"Murray Glick?"

Sussman thought he could hear Susie's cute little nose twisting in disgust. "Murray was the one who wanted to see the coat in the first place, Suse. He really ought to be there."

An exasperated sigh filtered through the telephone. "Andy, I was planning on spending tomorrow morning sound asleep, then waking up at ten, fixing myself a nice cup of coffee, doing my nails, and finishing a book I started

146

last July. Instead, as a pure favor to you, I'm going to wake up at six, slog down to the police station, and if that's not bad enough, I've got to have Murray Glick leering at me.''

"I promise he'll be on his good behavior, Susie.''

"I'll bet. I'm bringing my Mace anyway.''

"We'll be in a police station!''

"You can't be too careful.''

"All right, all right. Seven-fifteen, we'll meet you at Ashland Avenue. I promise I'll keep Murray in line. We'll go to Gritzbe's afterwards and have breakfast, okay? I'll treat.''

"Fine,'' Susie said. "I've got to run now. I'm going home to get some sleep.''

"You're still at the office?''

"Of course; how do you think I got tomorrow off?''

"What a life. Hey, Susie, thanks a lot.''

"No problem. See you tomorrow, Andy.''

"G'night, Suse.'' Sussman hung up the phone and turned back to Freddie Granger, who was being interrogated by Murray.

"I'm never down here at four,'' Granger was saying. "I eat early, so I can be around when the players start coming in. Some of those guys need a couple hours to get taped or loosen up; then there's Bryce and his goddamn chanting. . . .''

"So when Señor Flame called, the night he hurt his knee, you would have been out eating?'' Murray asked.

"Yeah, that's right.''

"And somebody else would have answered the phone and left you the message?''

"Right . . . no, wait.'' Granger wound up some loose tape and stuck it in a drawer. "As a matter of fact, they didn't leave a message. One of the maintenance guys answered Flame's call, thought it was important, so he called me right away. I always leave a number when I go out, in case someone gets hurt.''

"Do you remember who the maintenance guy was?''

"Nah. Could've been anybody. It's mostly temporary help.''

"Do you remember where you were eating?'' Sussman asked.

"Yeah, I was at Hathaway's. I was sitting at the bar, having a hamburger when the bartender shoves me the phone. It was pretty funny, actually. There's a lot of guys come in there, got action on the games, right? So I say, 'Hey, fellas, here's a hot tip. The Flames are missing a key man, tonight'—and a few heads turn so's I can see who's got bets down—and I say, 'Señor Flame hurt his knee—he's out for a week!' I thought that was pretty funny, but a few of the guys in there weren't amused. I thought the guy next to me was gonna dump his ketchup bottle in my lap.''

"Freddie,'' Murray said, "do you recall who was there at Hathaway's that night when you got the phone call?''

Granger shrugged. "I'm not sure, really. Lester hadn't showed up yet. Charlie, the bartender, a few other guys.''

"Would you remember if you saw them again?''

"I don't know. Probably not.'' Granger looked at his watch. "It's getting late, fellas. We've got another game tomorrow, I'm going to have some sore players to take care of in the morning.''

"Okay, Freddie, we're done,'' Sussman said. "We've got an early-morning date tomorrow, ourselves.''

"We do?'' said Murray.

"We're meeting Susie Ettenger at the Ashland Avenue police station. We're going to let you model an overcoat.''

"Aha!'' Murray leered at Sussman as they left Granger and headed back upstairs. "Breakfast with Susie! That's great, Hoops.''

148

"Yeah, well, the sergeant wants us in early, otherwise we'll have to wait until Monday."

"No, I mean for you and Susie. When was the last time you saw her?"

"Murray, I'm warning you, if you say one thing tomorrow . . ."

"Andrew, you've got to keep after a girl like her! I think it's time to make your move, time to take her out for a night on the town. In fact, maybe you can double-date with Wendy and me."

"Murray!"

"What?"

"Don't even think about it."

"Why not?"

"Murray . . ." Sussman took his wool stocking cap, stuffed it on Murray's head, and pulled it down over Murray's face.

"Hey!" protested Glick, through the hat. "Whfr ew—"

"I promised Susie you'd be on your best behavior, Mr. Glick, and that's one promise I intend to keep."

"Hpps—"

"Time to go home, Murray." Sussman zipped his parka and pulled on his gloves. "Say good night to the guard." He grabbed Murray's arm and waved it at the security guard who was stationed by the press entrance.

"G'night, fellas," the guard said.

"Wrfgl, Hpps."

Sussman pointed Murray outside; then, feeling the wind whipping past his ears, he took his stocking cap back and pulled it on. He gave Murray instructions to meet him at his apartment at 6:30 the next morning, found his Datsun at the end of the parking lot, and drove off into the frigid Chicago night.

18

IT WAS A RAINY, windswept morning, the kind that happens several times a winter in Chicago when the temperature rises enough to melt the snow, blending it with the dirt and the soot, turning the streets into rivers of gray slush. Andy Sussman was sitting in the passenger seat of Murray Glick's red Maserati; they were dodging potholes on Ashland Avenue, heading south toward the police station.

"Wait'll Susie sees this," Murray said, slowing down as they reached the driveway. "In fact, I'll let you drive it over to breakfast afterwards if you want—you can tell her you're going to buy it from me."

"Murray, I don't think Susie's the type of girl who'll be bowled over by a used Maserati."

"Ah, Andy, you give women too much credit. All this feminist crap they've been shoveling at you. Now, you take Susie Ettenger. There's a girl who spends six days a week acting professional, working herself to the bone—take my word for it, Hoops, she doesn't want equal treatment from you. She wants a little flash, a little style. Take the Maz, treat her to dinner—take her to Vegas for the weekend, I bet she'd love that."

"Murray, do you think it's possible to forget about my

love life for a few minutes and concentrate on solving this case, just in case I ever feel like resuming my career?''

"Fine, fine. Die a lonely man." Murray parked the car in front of the Ashland Avenue police station, a two-storied gray building, lost in a gray street on a gray day. Even the blue-and-white police cars looked faded, splashed with grime and dirty snow. "There she is," Murray said, as a beige Oldsmobile Cutlass pulled up behind them. "Comb your hair, Andy."

Sussman ran his hand over his hair and pulled on his wool cap.

"A stocking cap? Andrew, that's awfully low-rent." Murray pulled out a furry Russian hat. "Here, wear this."

"Mur—"

"For you, Hoops. For you, I risk pneumonia."

"Keep your hat, Murray." Sussman stepped out of the car and slogged through the slush, toward the Cutlass; he found Susie Ettenger huddled inside, sipping some coffee. "Morning, Suse," he said, opening the door.

"Hi, Andy," yawned Susie. "I guess it is morning, all right. Oh God . . ." She looked up and saw the door swing open on Murray's Maserati. "He's got the heavy artillery out. I'm telling you, Andy, if that guy makes one false move, I'm going to dump this coffee right down his crotch."

"Aw, come on, Susie, give him a chance." Sussman took Susie's hand and helped her out of the car. "He's really not such a bad guy, and he's doing this for free, you know."

"Just keep him out of my reach."

"Susela!" Murray Glick, striding over from the Maserati, slipped his spidery frame between Sussman and Susie. "Susie Ettenger, I haven't seen you since Sherry Dansworth's Christmas party. What you been up to, kid? You look great."

"Nothing much, Murray, just the usual. Weekend flings to Mexico, nights on Rush Street, a few tawdry affairs. I practice a little law."

"Ah, Susie, what a kidder." Murray started to put his arm around Susie, but she slipped deftly away.

"I'd just as soon not catch pneumonia out here," Susie said. "It's seven-twenty. Let's go inside, they ought to be here by now."

Sussman, Susie, and Murray walked into the police station, where a stout desk sergeant greeted them. "G'morning, folks. What can I do for you?"

"My name's Susan Ettenger. We're here to see Sergeant Granville," Susie said. "He's expecting us."

The officer checked his ledger. "Let's see . . ."

"It's okay, let them back," wheezed a voice from behind. A series of hacking coughs ensued, followed by a futile attempt at throat clearing. *"A-aack,"* coughed Detective Lafferty, stepping forward. "Good morning, Mr. Sussman. Good morning, Miss Ellerman." He looked over at Murray Glick.

"Good morning, Detective," Murray said, sticking out his right hand. "My name's Steven Feinberg. I'm from the American Civil Liberties Union. I'm involved with Mr. Sussman as an *amicus curiae—*"

"I wonder if we could get going," interrupted Susie. "I know we all have other things to do today."

"Amicus what?" said Lafferty.

"Friend of the court," Murray explained. "In re Mr. Sussman's defamation-of-character suit against WCGO. We suspect his civil rights may have been violated."

"He's here strictly for observation," Sussman said. "Honestly, Detective Lafferty, we're doing everything we can to expedite your case, and naturally to clear my own name—"

Lafferty let out a twenty-one–gun cough and motioned

his three visitors toward a metal cage at the back of the police station. He gave a form to a uniformed policeman who was standing duty inside and waited silently as the man retrieved Lester Beldon's overcoat. "You'll have to examine the coat right here," Lafferty said. "I'll stay and observe."

"Here we are," said the man in the cage. He handed over a brown winter coat, creased and dusty from the several weeks it had lain stashed in the cubicle. "Sign here, please."

Susie Ettenger signed the form and took the coat over to an empty wooden desk.

"We pulled the personal belongings out of the pockets, of course," said Lafferty. "I believe you were given a copy of the contents, Miss Ellerman."

"Ettenger," Susie said. "Yes, we have the list."

"And you'll note the blood stains. When the deceased was shot, he fell backward, as I'm sure Mr. Sussman recalls, staining the coat, which was folded on the chair."

"Right," said Sussman. He felt slightly queasy; the last time he had seen the overcoat, Lester Beldon's body had been slumped against it, his life draining away.

"Excuse me," Murray said, wedging himself between Sussman and Susie. "If you don't mind, these things always interest me."

"I didn't realize ACLU lawyers were such experts at examining evidence," Detective Lafferty said.

Murray ignored Lafferty and ran his fingers over the front of the coat, handling the garment like a magician. He felt inside the pockets, twisted the buttons, turned the coat inside out. Then he inspected the lining.

"Incidentally," Sussman said, trying to divert Lafferty's attention from Murray—he assumed Murray was doing nothing illegal, but then with Murray, you never assumed anything—"I think we have a pretty good idea how the murder was committed."

Lafferty jerked his head around.

"I mean, we're fairly certain that whoever did it was dressed in Señor Flame's uniform."

"Señor who? What are you talking about?"

"Señor Flame, the team mascot. He dances around during games dressed in a Flame costume, but the night of the murder he was in the hospital. The Phoenix announcer said he saw Señor Flame dancing on the floor right before the lights went out, though."

"The *Phoenix* announcer? There were five-thousand people in the Stadium that night, Mr. Sussman. Didn't any of them see this, uh . . ."

"Mascot? Well, the thing is, Detective, they wouldn't have noticed anything unusual, because Señor Flame's there every night. Although that particular night—"

"Ahem," said Murray, leaning over the coat.

"Did anyone see him with a gun?" asked Lafferty.

"No . . ."

"And the only person who can assure us that he was there at all is this guy in Phoenix?"

"Excuse me, Detective," said Murray, standing up straight.

Detective Lafferty wheezed and looked at Glick.

"I think you should take a look at this." Murray turned the overcoat inside out and spread it over the table. He grabbed the right inner lining and held it, tentlike, under the fluorescent lights. "Notice anything unusual here?"

Lafferty hunched over the table and examined the lining, while Sussman and Susie Ettenger peered over his shoulder. "It looks like it may have been removed once or twice."

"Once or twice? Look at this." Murray shook the lining and lifted it to Lafferty's eye level. "Look at the threads here, Detective.'' The thread connecting the lining to the jacket was darker than the rest of the threading, and it had been sewn on clumsily. Several short strands of thread had been cut short and left hanging. "This lining has been sewn in and out at least a dozen times," Murray said. "Here, they used the left side a few times, too." He held the left side of the jacket to the light. "I'm surprised the coat held up at all."

Lafferty picked up the overcoat and held the lining so that the light shined through the clumsy threading. "This is an old coat," he said. "As you probably know, Mr. Sussman, Lester Beldon was in the habit of hanging on to his possessions for unusually long periods of time. Every article of clothing we found on him was at least three years old."

"Actually," Sussman said, "I don't think our friend Mr. Feinberg was disputing the age of the clothes."

"The point is," Lafferty said, "that given Mr. Beldon's noted thriftiness, it doesn't seem extraordinary that he might have made several attempts to repair the lining."

"This is no coincidence," Murray said. "On twenty-seven different occasions, from the season's start until the day Lester Beldon was murdered, this coat was used as a medium of exchange, probably between Beldon and whoever killed him."

"Is that right? And I suppose you have evidence of that?"

"I have over a hundred hours of videotape, Detective. I've seen that coat hanging over Lester's chair one moment, gone the next, then back again. Something illegal, probably drugs, was being sewn into that lining. Lester would leave the coat on his chair while he taped the pre-game interview—that would be a couple of hours before the game, there'd be all types of unofficial people wandering around. While Lester was doing his interview, his partner comes, switches coats, goes into a washroom or who knows where, takes the drugs out of Lester's lining, slips in the payment, and switches the coats back.''

"That's pretty detailed analysis for a 'friend of the court,' isn't it?'' Lafferty asked.

"I'm only concerned with protecting Mr. Sussman's rights,'' said Murray. "If the evidence is obvious that the murder was committed by someone else—''

"Obvious?'' Lafferty held up the coat again, then tossed it onto the table. "What you've got here, Mr. Feinberg, is a moth-eaten old jacket. You say it was sewn up by some drug dealers, I say it could have been repaired by anyone. You've got some videotapes which may or may not show the jacket being taken—I'll have to see them for myself—and then there's this TV announcer in Phoenix who says he saw the team mascot, but nobody who was at the game can remember whether he was really there or not. . . .'' Lafferty pulled out a small spiral notebook. "I suppose we could check the uniform for gunpowder burns, if your Mister Flame hasn't washed it or thrown it away.''

"He bought a new uniform last week,'' Sussman said, staring at the floor. "Last night was his big comeback. I don't know if he kept the old one.''

"That's hardly overwhelming evidence, then. And you have absolutely no clue as to who this alleged drug dealer is, who was supposedly connected to Lester Beldon?''

"May I remind you, Detective,'' said Susie Ettenger, "that it's not the job of Mr. Sussman to solve your cases for you. I believe we've been more than cooperative in passing along the evidence we've obtained; now in the interest of getting this case quickly resolved—''

"Miss Ellenger,'' said Lafferty, "the Chicago Police Department welcomes the involvement of any concerned citizen in regard to an unsolved crime. But even if Mr. Feinberg's theory is true, Mr. Sussman still remains a suspect. Certainly if drugs were involved, he would have as easy access to them as Mr. Beldon, probably easier, considering Mr. Sussman's well-known associations with many of the players on the team.''

"What's that supposed to mean?'' snapped Sussman.

"Ahem . . . ,'' Murray said, elbowing Sussman in the ribs.

"I don't think I need to elaborate on the habits of the current generation of professional basketball players.''

"Detective Lafferty,'' said Sussman, "I have not, and have never had, any dealings with drugs or drug dealers. I'm a professional, and I have a career to protect, despite your best efforts to destroy it.''

"Ahem!'' Murray stepped between Sussman and Detective Lafferty. "I don't think Mr. Sussman means to dispute your analysis,'' he said. "In fact, it's the basis for everything that happened to the unfortunate Mr. Beldon. We'd certainly encourage you to increase your investigation of drug use around the team, Detective; as our client is entirely uninvolved, your efforts can only lead to the eventual apprehension of the real killer.''

Lafferty shifted glances from Murray to Sussman—it was unclear who he trusted less—then gave the coat a cursory reexamination. "We can certainly take that into consideration. Now, if the three of you are finished . . .''

"I believe we found what we were looking for,'' said Murray.

"Good.'' Lafferty picked up the coat and returned it to the cage.

"Jesus, Murray,'' muttered Sussman, "thanks a lot.''

"Shush,'' said Murray. "Don't piss off anybody else around here, Hoops. We got what we wanted, and we still need their help. Come on, let's make tracks.'' He put his arm around Susie. "Did I hear something about a free

breakfast at Gritzbe's, courtesy of an out-of-work basketball announcer?''

Susie tried to squirm out of Murray's grip.

''Susela, I'll bet you look even more beautiful after
some lox and bagels and a hot cup of coffee.''

''Murray—'' Susie shook off Glick's arm.

''C'mon, sweetheart,'' Murray said, patting her on the
behind and grabbing her arm again.

''Ahem.'' Susie smiled at Murray, turned around, and
politely whispered into his ear. ''Rape.''

''Pardon me?'' Murray said.

''Rape,'' Susie whispered again.

''What's with you two lovebirds?'' said Sussman.
''Leaving me out of some strategy?''

Murray unwrapped his arm and buried it in his pocket.

''Actually,'' Susie said, ''I was just mentioning to Mr.
Feinberg that I had some pressing business to attend to.''

''Aw, I thought you were going to let me buy you
breakfast.''

''Maybe you and Murray should discuss the nonlegal
aspects of this case by yourselves.'' Susie zipped up her
coat. ''Call me this afternoon, okay, Andy? Maybe we
can have brunch tomorrow and figure out where things
stand.''

''Sure thing, Susie.''

''Good-bye, Murray,'' Susie said icily. She tossed her
purse over her shoulder, headed back toward the sergeant's desk and out the front door.

''Nice seeing you again, sweetheart,'' shouted Murray.
He turned back to Sussman. ''Geez, Hoopsie, she's a
tough one. I might have trouble getting used to a girl like
that.''

''I don't think it's a problem you'll have to deal with
right away. Come on, Mur, let's get out of here.''

They left the police station, climbed into Murray's Maserati, and headed back to Sussman's apartment. "Murray," Sussman said, fastening his shoulder harness, "how in the world do you expect anyone to believe that Lester Beldon was running a drug ring? Honestly, the guy didn't even chew gum."

"Who knows? Maybe he was having some financial problems."

"We checked his financial records. No large cash withdrawals, no suspicious activities—the guy was clean."

"Well, maybe he had some rare disease or something and needed the money."

"Uh huh, sure."

"Hoops, there are a hundred things that could make a guy need cash all of a sudden. Maybe he was betting on the games, maybe he got a girl in trouble. What if he had another kid somewhere from a one-night stand? Hell, Andy, he played for ten years in a lot of tank towns. What if he was being blackmailed? Maybe he figures if he could just score one quick cocaine deal, he'd be set. He makes a fast half mil, puts it in a bank somewhere, and pays off whoever it was—"

"Pure speculation, Murray."

"Could be, Hoops. Or maybe Lester just liked the stuff. There's no profile for using drugs, you know. Just because a guy is a cheap, obnoxious jerk doesn't mean he can't get a little high once in a while." Murray turned off Fullerton, onto Parkview. "You know what, Andy?"

"What, Murray?"

"Remember that appointment with the dermatologist that Lester had scheduled, the card they found in his pocket?"

"Yeah."

"I think we ought to check it out. You think that guy works on Saturdays?"

"He's in Wilmette, if I remember it right. Suburban

offices are usually open for a few hours on Saturdays. I don't know what you're expecting to find, though.''

"Who knows? Maybe he's fixing up noses on the side, maybe he was some kind of contact.''

"Right, Murray. Or maybe he's just taking care of some cheerleader's zits.''

"Think positive, Hoops.'' Murray pulled into Sussman's parking lot and turned off the engine. "It's a quarter to nine. Think they'll be in by ten o'clock?''

"There's one way to find out. I've got the doctor's name written down in my desk.''

"Well, go upstairs and give him a call. We'll go out for breakfast, then head over.'' Murray pulled a pineapple swirl from his glove compartment, unwrapped the plastic, and swallowed half of it in one gulp. "And step on it,'' he said as Sussman made his way through the slush, toward the front entrance of his apartment building. "I'm starved.''

19

THE LEHMAN MEDICAL CENTER was a shiny three-storied building, made of steel and glass and shaped like a U, with a parking area between the two wings. Sussman and Glick entered at the center door and matched the name from Lester Beldon's appointment card—Dr. Cecil Montague—with an office on the third floor. They took the elevator up, got out, and stood in the hallway, surveying the situation.

"Remember, you're Charles Hirsch," Murray said, stopping in front of a tinted-glass door that read: "302: Lehman Dermatologists' Group."

"Gotcha," said Sussman, adjusting the phony mustache Murray had given him. Being a radio announcer, Sussman had never had to worry much about public visibility, but since Lester's death, his picture had been in the papers and on television several times, and he did not want to take any chances.

"Aha!" said Murray, strolling past the office entrance, stopping at another door that was unmarked and locked. "This could be the place. They probably sneak the nose patients in the side office, then let 'em out through this door."

"Murray, all doctors' offices take up more than one room. I'm sure they just keep it locked all the time."

"We'll see, Hoops. C'mon." Murray led Sussman inside the doctors' office. It was 10:15 and they had just opened;

several patients sat in the waiting room, most of them with some type of visible skin ailment. Sussman did not see anyone who looked as though he might be waiting to have his nose fixed.

"Can I help you?" a receptionist asked.

"Mr. Mordecai and Mr. Hirsch, here to see Doctor Montague."

The receptionist looked at her appointment book.

"Actually, we don't have an appointment," Murray said. "We're from the American Association of Dermatologists; we're doing a little spot check of some of the newer facilities in the area. We'll only be a few minutes."

"Hmm," said the receptionist. "Just a second, I'll buzz Doctor Montague. He's got a full slate today, but maybe he can spare a few minutes."

Sussman and Glick waited briefly, until a tall man in a white smock appeared in the receptionist's window. "Good morning, gentlemen," he said. He was slim, in his late fifties, with a sparse shock of brown hair and a pallid complexion. It occurred to Sussman that he would have more confidence in a dermatologist with a nice golden suntan, but all the ones he had ever met looked as if they had not been out of the lab since they'd graduated from medical school. "I'm Doctor Montague," the man announced. "What can I do for you?"

Murray repeated his desire to investigate the facilities, and Dr. Montague, after peering at his schedule, motioned them inside. "I wish you'd given me some advance warning," he said. "Why don't you step back here, I'll give you a quick tour; then I've got to get back to my patients."

"Thank you, Doctor," said Murray.

"We've just ordered two new UV lamps," Montague said, leading Sussman and Murray into a small room with a table, an elevated bed, and a sunlamp. "They should be in next week."

"We'd love to see them," Murray said, "but, as I'm sure you can appreciate, the nature of the inspections are such that we can't give any advance warning." He walked out of the little room, craning his neck down the hall.

"There's three other rooms like that one," Montague said. "They're all about the same, I don't think there's any reason to go inside."

"We'd just like to take a peek," Murray said. "Nothing personal, of course, just procedural rules."

Dr. Montague shrugged. He knocked on the closed door of one of the rooms, marked "B."

"Yes?" said a voice.

"Mrs. Flanders, it's Doctor Montague. Are you dressed yet?"

"I just have to put my shoes back on. You can come in."

Dr. Montague opened the door. A frumpy woman in her late forties was inside, lacing up a pair of shoe boots; she did not look like a candidate for a deviated septum operation. "Satisfied?" asked the doctor. He moved to the next office, where a young boy was lying under a sunlamp. The third room was empty.

"What about down there?" Murray asked. He walked down the hallway toward a locked room, which Sussman guessed fronted the locked, unmarked door.

"That's the lab," said Dr. Montague, in a voice suggesting that someone from the American Association of Dermatologists ought to be able to guess where the laboratory was.

"Right," Murray said. "We know it's a lab. We'd just like to take a look inside."

"Fine." Montague, his brow beginning to wrinkle, unlocked the door to the lab. The wall beside the entrance was filled with shelves and bookcases. The opposite wall, which covered the locked hallway door, was fronted by a small freezer and a table with three microscopes on it. "I'd really appreciate it if you didn't stay in here long,'' Montague said. ''We've had some insurance problems, and we can't have outside people handling anything.''

''Doctor Montague,'' announced a voice from the intercom. ''Doctor Montague, call on line three.''

''Just a second,'' Montague said. ''Could you wait outside, please? I'll be right back.'' He locked the laboratory door and walked into his private office to take the phone call.

''Well, so much for your 'Doctor Toot' theory,'' said Sussman. ''There's no nose work going on in here, unless they're doing it in the john.''

''C'mon, Hoops, use your imagination. They could do that operation in any of those little rooms. Have Lester walk in with a fake pimple, lie him down on one of those tables . . .''

''You're stretching, Mur. C'mon, let's get out of here.''

''Just a second,'' Murray said, grabbing Sussman by the arm.

''What now?''

''Don't you want to know what was wrong with Lester's skin?''

''Gentlemen,'' said Dr. Montague, holding a clipboard as he rejoined them. ''Is there anything else you'd like to see? I'm really quite busy here; if you want to wait until two o'clock—''

''Doctor Montague,'' said Murray, ''we only need about two more minutes of your time. Could we talk in private?''

Dr. Montague looked at his watch.

''This won't take long.''

''I'm really pressed for time.''

''Just two minutes.''

Montague dropped his hands, letting the clipboard bump against his knee. ''Two minutes,'' he said, leading Sussman and Glick back to his private office.

''Now, Doctor Montague,'' Murray said, glancing around

the room, "I have a slight confession to make. Mr. Hirsch and I aren't actually from the American Association of Dermatologists—"

Montague slammed his clipboard on his desk and stood up. "All right," he said, pointing to the door, "out! I thought you guys were phonies from the start—"

"Wait, wait." Murray stood his ground, holding his arm out to ward off the doctor. "Actually, we are legitimate, Doctor Montague. The thing is, we're insurance investigators."

Montague grimaced and sunk back into his chair.

"Cheer up, Doctor, we're not from your insurance company. We're from Sunbelt Mutual; we insure a patient of yours named Lester Beldon."

"Did insure," Montague said. "In case you haven't heard . . ."

"Yes, yes, of course, it was a real tragedy. Unfortunately, that's the nature of our visit."

Sussman, wary that Montague might make some image associations after hearing Beldon's name, rested his hand over his mustache and slumped back in the doctor's couch.

"It so happens," Murray continued, "that a week ago we received a claim from Mr. Beldon regarding several visits he had here in January."

"That's right," said Montague. "He came in several times."

"Well, Doctor Montague, because the claims came in two weeks after Mr. Beldon's ill-timed demise, it was necessary for us to come in and check their validity. We realize that the mail can be slow, but there's always the chance someone in the family might have forged the claim slips—you know, dire financial straits, that kind of thing."

"Gentlemen, I can assure you the visits were authentic."

"Very good, Doctor." Murray scribbled something down in a small notebook. "Now, if you could just quickly look up your records and explain the nature of the visits, then give us a photocopy to take back to the home office . . .''

"All right, fine." Dr. Montague buzzed his secretary. "Stella, could you please pull the file on Lester Beldon. I think it's under 'Dead Accounts.' " Montague smiled sheepishly. "We put all ex-patients in that category."

"I'm sure you do," Murray said.

A few moments later, Dr. Montague's receptionist returned with Lester's file. "Hmm," said Montague, scanning the report. "Yes, now I remember. This was quite an interesting case. Mr. Beldon had a recurring case of contact dermatitis—it had come back for the first time in over twenty-five years, but that was definitely what it was."

"Contact dermatitis?" Murray asked.

"It's a skin ailment—actually closer to an allergy. It can lead to rashes around the back, neck, and arms, wherever the skin comes into contact with the contaminating agent. Mr. Beldon first experienced the ailment in, let's see . . ." Dr. Montague flipped through the file. "Nineteen fifty-seven. It was just after the birth of his second child. Lots of things can cause rashes, of course, but in Lester's case, it turned out to be some detergent—no wait. . . ." He gave the file a closer look. "No, it was the powder he was putting on his baby's diapers. He was using that 20 Mule Team Borax, or whatever they call it—you know, the stuff Reagan used to shill for on 'Death Valley Days'?"

"Borax?" said Sussman. "On diapers?"

"That's right. People used it as a baby powder then. I think the Beldons were using it as a laundry detergent, too. Lester would get the stuff all over his hands when he changed diapers or did the laundry, and the result was a long rash, chafing on his hands." Montague looked up from the report. "Once we detected it, he stopped using the borax—or let Shirley change the diapers—and the rash went away. It stayed away, too, for years. Then one day he comes into the office—"

"Do you remember what day that was?" Murray asked.

The doctor looked at his report. "December twelfth, of last fall. 'Patient complaining of rashes under his arms, chafing, etc. . . . Diagnosed as contact dermatitis. Patient can't recall using borax. Unable to find other causes for inflammation . . .' " He put the report down. "That was the strange part, Mr. Mordecai. We made all sorts of tests to see what might be causing the rash, but nothing else showed up. Furthermore, certain dry, abrasive spots near his hips definitely indicated that the borax, or something chemically similar, could have been present."

"Hmm," said Murray. "Dr. Montague, did the borax have to be spread all over Lester's body for it to cause the infection?"

"No, just a little bit seemed to do it. The skin gets irritated, a rash breaks out—it's sort of like poison ivy in that respect." He skimmed through the rest of the report. "Does that help you any?"

"That's extremely helpful. I think we can say without any doubt that the claims were legitimate. Right, Mr. Hirsch?"

"Right," mumbled Sussman.

"In that case, if I can get back to my patients . . ."

"Of course. Thanks so much for your time, Doctor, you've been a great help." Murray rose from his chair and pointed Sussman out of the office.

"Well, that was certainly fascinating," Sussman said, as they collected a copy of Beldon's medical records and walked back into the hall. "Maybe Lester was dying of terminal dermatitis."

"Andrew . . ."

"Maybe he was so distraught that he hired someone to kill him, so he wouldn't have to go through the agony."

167

"Hoops . . ." Murray led Sussman into an empty elevator and pushed the button for the lobby.

"The poor guy, Mur. He must have figured, why go on? Why go through thousands of dollars in dermatologists' bills—*hey!*"

The elevator rocked to a halt, tossing Sussman to the floor. "Murray! What the hell . . ."

Murray held his finger against the emergency stop button. "Andrew," he said, "listen to me."

"Jesus, Murray, get your finger off the goddamn button."

"Hoops," Murray said, as the emergency buzzer reverberated through the elevator, "think: what's borax?"

"I know what borax is, Murray. I watched 'Death Valley Days.' "

"C'mon, Hoops. What else is it? White. Dry. Powdery. What's it used for besides laundry detergent?"

"Murray, I know what you're getting at, but why would Lester go to the doctor for a problem if he knew what was causing it? What if he just started using a new detergent and didn't know what was in it? He gets a little on his hands, a rash breaks out . . ."

Murray frowned and held the emergency button, as the buzzer continued to screech. "Think a little harder, Hoops."

Sussman pulled his hat over his ears and sank back into the corner of the elevator. "Okay, okay, Murray, turn the goddamn thing off already, will you? Borax can be used to cut cocaine."

Murray took his thumb off the emergency button; the buzzer stopped, and the elevator resumed its downward path.

"But honestly, Mur, don't you think you're going a little far with this? I mean, even if Lester was cutting cocaine with borax, why keep insisting to Doctor Montague that he wasn't using it at all?" The elevator opened at the first floor; Sussman followed Murray off it and headed toward the parking lot. "And why keep coming back here if he knew what was causing the problem?"

"Because," Murray said, as they approached the Maserati, "maybe Lester didn't know what was causing the problem?"

"Didn't know? What do you mean, how could he not know?"

"Maybe he didn't know that the cocaine was being cut. Maybe it was being done behind his back. Maybe he didn't even know—"

"Watch out!!"

A sharp ping sounded a few inches from Murray's ear.

"Hoops—get down!" Murray dived behind his car, pulling Sussman along with him.

"What the fuck!" Sussman covered his face as he hit the ground. Another ping was heard, then a shattering of glass from the front of the car.

"Damn it!" Murray said, looking up for a moment, then ducking his head underneath the fender as another shot rang out.

"Murray—"

Glick and Sussman lay quietly on the ground for about thirty seconds, tasting crumbled pebbles of asphalt. Then, about fifty yards away, an engine roared; Sussman looked up and saw a red Camaro screech out of the parking lot and pull away. "Murray?" he said, reaching over to his friend. A small crowd was starting to gather a few yards from the Maserati. "Murray, are you—"

"Jesus Christ . . ." Murray got up slowly and dusted himself off. "Look at this jacket . . ." He knelt on the asphalt and ran his hand beneath the right rear tire. "I told you at the start, Hoops, I don't take cases like this anymore."

"Murray, I'm not crazy about getting shot at, either."

"Murders, Hoops, I don't need that." Murray surveyed the ground behind the rear bumper and groped underneath the transmission. "I've got a nice practice now, Andy," he said. "I can wear a suit to work. I can get life insurance. For you, Hoops; for you I'm doing this. . . ."

"I appreciate it, Murray, believe me."

Murray got up, walked over to the front of his car, and cleared the broken glass out of the right headlight.

"At least we know someone's suspicious," Sussman said. "We must be getting close."

Murray got down on his knees again and began scouring the asphalt. "Yeah, too close." He ran his hand over a bullet mark above the right front fender.

"Someone had to have been following us all morning, Murray. Maybe since last night."

Murray bent over and looked underneath the tail pipe.

"What's the matter, Murray?" said Sussman. "You lose a contact?"

"Here!" Murray said. He picked up a melted lead slug from underneath the exhaust and held it up to the light.

"Good eye, Mur." Sussman reached for the slug, but Murray pulled it back. "You want me to send that to Susie? Maybe she can get a ballistics report."

"Nope." Murray took the slug and dropped it in his coat pocket. "Matching paperweights, Andrew. A memento of my last murder case." He patted the pocket, then got back into the Maserati. "C'mon," he said, turning the ignition. "Enough for one morning. It's lunch time, pal, let's get the hell out of here."

20

"ALL RIGHT, HOOPS, try it again, this time with the knife in your pocket."

Sussman placed the Swiss Army knife in the pocket of his slacks and walked through the doorless entrance to Murray's Northbrook Court detective agency. As he did so, a buzzer blasted out, startling several ladies who were sampling chocolate peanut clusters at Fannie Mae's. "I think it's working," he shouted.

"Okay," Murray yelled back, from inside his office. "Try it once more now, without the knife."

Sussman flipped the pocketknife over the top of the metal detector, so that it landed on the receptionist's desk, and walked back across the newly activated threshold. The alarm was silent. "Looks like it's all set, Murray. Can I come inside?"

"Yeah, yeah. Come on in, Hoops."

Sussman twisted the knob on Murray's inner-office door, but could not get it to turn. "Murray!" he shouted. He heard a loud, electronic click.

"Okay, try it now."

Sussman pushed the door open and found Murray leaning back on his leather swivel chair, smoking a cigar, looking at a TV monitor which displayed the entrance to the storefront. "Honestly, Murray, don't you think you're overdoing it a little?"

Murray tapped an ash into the large ceramic ashtray on his desk. "You think so, Hoops? You like being shot at?"

"No, I don't like being shot at. I just don't think someone's going to march into the middle of Northbrook Court and open fire on us."

"Andrew, may I remind you we're talking about murderers, here? People who kill other people can't always be expected to behave in a conventional manner." Murray took the lead slug out of his pocket and set it next to his paperweight. "Take a seat, Hoops, we've got a few things to go over."

Sussman pulled aside one of Murray's plush leather chairs and sat down. "Look, Murray, it's pretty obvious that somewhere along the line we've gotten too close to the truth."

"One step at a time, Andrew. First, let's fit the new pieces into the puzzle." Murray grabbed a remote-control unit and flicked on his VCR. It was frozen on Lester Beldon giving one of his halftime interviews, with his overcoat in the upper left-hand corner of the screen. "This is December eleventh, the day before Lester went into Montague's office to complain about his rash." Murray advanced the tape to show the coat disappearing, then reappearing again. "This would have been the day they started cutting the cocaine. It's hardly the start of the exchange, though. . . ." Murray put in another tape. "We can see the coat exchange happening here, and in seven other games dating back to the third home game of the season. So let's say Lester started selling cocaine at that game. He was raking in the dough, but after a couple of weeks he—or someone else—got greedy. They started cutting the coke with borax to make it last longer and keep the money coming in. Giving Lester the benefit of the doubt, let's say he had a partner—and this partner, whoever he was, didn't tell Lester he was diluting the product. He kept the excess coke for himself, maybe used it or sold it and kept the profits. Meanwhile, the coat's still being used for the exchange, and somewhere along the line a little of the product leaks out and touches Lester's skin—it wouldn't have taken much. That would explain why Lester didn't know what was causing his rash.''

"Having a partner makes sense to me," said Sussman. "I can't imagine Lester would have actually been friendly with anyone who dealt coke; but if he wanted to make a quick deal, he would have known someone who *did* know, just from being around the league."

"I'll buy that," Murray said. "So let's reset the scenario. Lester calls up his partner, who arranges the cocaine deal; we'll call him Mr. X. Everything's going fine for a couple of weeks, until Mr. X decides he can play fat old Lester for a sucker. And *then* . . .'' Murray took his gold lighter and relit his cigar. "Let's say the purchaser, Mr. P, discovers his product's been tampered with. He calls Mr. X to complain, and Mr. X, being no dummy, says *he* doesn't know anything about it. He wants to save *his* ass, right? So Mr. X says it must be Lester's doing. Mr. X skips town, and a few nights later, poor Lester Beldon—''

A buzzer blast shattered Murray's monologue and sent him scurrying back to his desk drawer. He pulled a revolver out and motioned Sussman to back away from the door.

"Murray, will you relax—''

"Get down, Hoops.''

"Murray!" screamed a high-pitched voice from outside.

"Jesus Christ," Murray said, staring at the image of Wendy Altman on the TV monitor. "What's she doing here?" He picked up his phone and buzzed his secretary.

"Peggy . . . Yes, I can see who it is. Tell her to walk back outside and take off her bracelets."

The alarm stopped.

"I forgot about her," Murray said, opening his appointment book. "I think we were supposed to have a late lunch somewhere. Maybe we can order something in." He pulled out a dozen menus from fast-food outlets in the mall and set them on his desk.

"Somehow, Mur, I don't think Wendy will find a Saturday lunch date at Mario's Piece-O-Pizza particularly romantic."

"Maybe she finds being shot at romantic?" Glick pushed the menus aside. "Look, Hoops, I'll take care of that broad, all right? Let's get your next move set up."

"*My* next move—"

The alarm went off again, followed by an even louder shriek.

"Mur-ray! Murray Glick!"

Murray picked up the phone. "Peggy. . . ." The alarm continued to sound. "Peggy, tell her to back out again and take her rings off, okay?" The buzzing went on unabated. "And her sunglasses."

The alarm stopped.

"Now, Hoops, as I was saying: I think it would be best if I lay low for a while."

"That's great, Murray. You're not the only one they were shooting at, you know."

"Andrew," Murray said, resting his cigar on the ashtray, "remember the terms upon which I took this case? If you'll recall, my contributions were supposed to be strictly analytical."

"Murray, we're so close to solving this thing—"

"Exactly. Which is why I don't want to take any needless risks. All you have to do is get a few answers for me, and we'll be able to close this case and get you back to work." Murray held up his legal pad. "First of all, I want the results from that drug test they took on all the players. Also, try and track down Señor Flame's old uniform, the one that should have the gunpowder burns on it. That's not so difficult."

"Mur-rrry!" screamed Wendy Altman, as the alarm blasted out again. "Murray will you *please* turn that thing off?"

Murray picked up his phone. "Peggy," he said, "what else is she wearing with metal in it . . . Earrings? Fine. . . . Her belt? . . . Peggy, have her go back outside, okay?"

The alarm became quiet.

"Now tell her to take off the earrings and the belt. . . ." Murray watched the monitor. "And her watch. . . ." He gnawed on his cigar. "An anklet? Yeah, that too." He hung up the phone. "Holy Toledo, Hoops, you could melt that girl down and use her to balance the trade deficit with Japan."

"I warned you to watch what you were getting into, Murray."

"Ah, don't worry, Hoops, I think I'm getting her under control." Murray picked up his legal pad. "Now, there's a few more facts we need to clear up before we can nail this guy, whoever he is. You know that girl who's been hanging around Sly Thomas the last few weeks? The one who didn't want him to go to that testimonial for Lester Beldon?"

"It's a memorial, Murray, not a testimonial."

"Whatever. I want to know who she is and what her relationship with Sly is. And I want you to double-check Shirley Beldon's alibi. Call that neighbor of hers, where she supposedly watched the game on cable the night Lester was shot. And double-check your list of sponsors—the ones he was supposed to meet with after the game."

"I've been through that list three times, Murray. No one remembers having any meeting set up with Lester that night."

Murray scratched his head. "That one throws me a little. I could understand someone setting up an appointment with Lester after the game, if that's when they meant to rub him out. But why set up a meeting for later, then murder him during the game—Sweet Jesus!" Murray choked on his cigar smoke as the alarm shrieked again. On the television monitor, he saw Wendy Altman take off her shoes and hurl them at his office door. The corresponding *whack* was heard a second later.

"Hell of a hummer," Sussman said as the telephone rang.

"Hello, Peggy . . . ," said Murray. "You think it's her *nail polish?*" Murray turned a lever underneath his desk drawer, and the buzzing stopped. "Okay, Peg, tell her she can put her things back on, I'll be right out." He hung up the phone. "So much for a five-thousand-dollar alarm system. Okay, Andrew, one more thing. Remember Señor Flame's phone call to Freddy Granger?"

"Right. . . ."

"Find out who answered it and relayed the message to Freddy. Then go back to Hathaway's and get a list of everyone who might have overheard Freddy say that Señor Flame was hurt, okay?"

"That may not be as easy as you think, Murray."

"Hoops, I have great faith in your investigative abilities."

"That really boosts my confidence, Mur."

"I expect a full report by Tuesday." Murray cuffed Sussman gently on the arm. "And give my best to Susie tomorrow, okay?"

"Susie?"

"Yeah. You're going out with her, remember? She said

'Call me Sunday, Andy, we'll have brunch.' Whatsamatter, kiddo, all this excitement get to your head?''

"Yeah, right, Murray. Thanks for the reminder." Sussman grabbed his jacket. "I'll be sure and give Susie your highest regards."

"Good." Murray hit a button under his desk, freeing the security lock on his office door, and led Sussman back outside.

"Murray!" screamed Wendy, her face red from hysterics. "Look what you *did* to me."

A small crowd had gathered outside the detective agency, watching Wendy and the pile of jewelry that was heaped on the floor outside the metal detector.

"Wendy, darling, I've had a rough day."

"Oh, yeah? Well, I've had a rough day, too. It's not every day you get strip-searched in front of your own boyfriend's office."

Sussman picked a loose earring off the floor and dropped it into Wendy's palm. "Very nice, Wendy. What is it, opal?"

"Obsidian," Wendy snapped. "Set in silver. I didn't realize I'd have to get them through the Secret Service."

"Take it easy, sweetheart," Murray said, fastening Wendy's necklace back on. "The First Lady goes through this every time she goes to the bathroom. I'm sure she doesn't complain."

"I'll bet."

"So long, Mur," Sussman said, waving at Murray as he strode out of the office.

"Talk to you Tuesday," said Murray, reattaching Wendy's silver anklet to her leg.

"Nice seeing you again, Wendy." Not waiting for a reply, Sussman walked over to the Fannie Mae candy store. He bought himself a chocolate turtle, popped it in his mouth, and ambled back into the mall.

21

"So, HOW'S YOUR hamburger?" Andy Sussman said to Susie Ettenger. It was noon, Sunday, and they were sitting at a musty table in the back of Hathaway's Pub.

"Mmm, delicious," Susie said, gently shaking her soft brown hair. "I especially like the way they shape the meat, so that it's exactly one half-inch bigger than the bun all the way around."

"Charlie's always been known for his symmetrical elegance, Suse." Sussman was relieved that Susie was accepting her date at Hathaway's with more grace than Wendy Altman had. Then again, he was not experiencing any perverse humor in the situation this time. He needed to check out the items on Murray's shopping list, and having Susie along seemed like a good idea. "Now, let's see," he said, referring to a note card, "do you think I need to follow up on those drug tests?"

"I'm pretty solid on that account. Bernie Chavous handles Jack Bryce's contract, he got the information this morning. They were all clean of coke and everything else, except for a little grass on a couple of the players, he wouldn't tell me which."

"Sly was clean, too?"

"Clean as a whistle. Of course, that has nothing to do

178

with whether he was dealing. The same goes with the rest of them.''

Sussman took a pen and drew a line through ''drug test.''

''Andy?'' Susie said, pushing her hamburger away.

''Yo.''

''Andy, did you find out any more about that network thing you were up for? You know, with Danny Borenstein?''

Sussman looked up curiously from his list and leaned toward Susie. ''Well, I think I've got a reasonably good chance of getting an assignment for one of the NCAA tournament games, if we can get this thing cleared up in the next week or so.''

''What about after that? Do you think they'd offer you a full-time network job?''

''I don't know, Suse. You mean in New York?''

''Well, yeah. I'm just curious about the type of terms they offer. You probably couldn't keep doing a full season of Flames games, could you? You'd probably have to move to New York.''

Oh boy, thought Sussman, as he stared into Susie's lovely brown eyes. Talk about painful choices: would it be New York and network glory versus Chicago and true love? ''Actually, it's mostly weekend work,'' he said. ''I think a lot of their guys stay in their home towns; some of them keep working locally.''

''Andy, how are ya!'' bellowed Charlie Hathaway, lumbering over to Sussman's table and wrapping a porcine arm over his neck. ''How come you're not in temple today, bubala?''

''We don't go to temple on Sunday, Charlie. We go on Friday nights.''

''Well, then, how was temple on Friday night?'' The

smoke from Charlie's omnipresent cigar drifted over Susie's hamburger. "And who's your gorgeous girlfriend?"

"I'm afraid I missed temple this week. And this is my attorney, Susan Ettenger. Ms. Ettenger, I'd like you to meet the proprietor of this establishment, Mr. Charles Hathaway."

"Pleased to meet you, Mr. Hathaway."

"Charlie, please. Wait a second . . ." Hathaway picked up Susie's water glass and inspected it under the dim lamp. "We want to make sure everything's clean around here, folks. We don't need any lawsuits. Arnie!" he shouted to the bartender. "Arnie, make sure you change the suds in the dishwasher today."

"Don't worry, Charlie," Sussman said. "We brought along purification tablets, just in case."

Hathaway tapped an ash into Sussman's butter dish, then surveyed the mostly empty restaurant. "So, what do you think, Suss? You think we can bring the Sunday brunch business back downtown?" He did a finger count of the nine people in the room. "This is my third week, now; I got new-style napkins, two-for-one on the beers, free fries with the cheeseburgers."

"Actually, Charlie," said Sussman, examining the battered piece of cardboard which listed the three forms of hamburgers available, "I think you may need to upgrade the menu a little."

"Why? What's wrong with hamburgers?"

"Nothing, Charlie. It's just that if people are going to come all the way out here for Sunday brunch, they might expect a bill of fare that's slightly more extravagant. Like maybe something with an egg in it."

"Hmph," said Hathaway. "Thirty years, I've been serving hamburgers. What'm I supposed to do, start dishing out crêpes?"

"You could always do something really drastic, like hire a cook."

Hathaway curled his lip and started to walk away.

"Hold on, Charlie."

"What?" Charlie waddled back. "The service isn't adequate, mon-sieur?"

"The service is fine. Listen, Charlie, I need to ask you a question. Remember the night Lester Beldon was murdered?"

"Aw, come on, Suss," Hathaway groaned. "Are we back on that again? I told you everything I knew."

"I'm just trying to jog your memory a little. Now think hard, Charlie: at about four-thirty that afternoon, before Lester came in, Freddy Granger was sitting at your bar eating dinner. You know, the trainer . . ."

"Yeah, sure, I know Freddy, he comes here a lot."

"Freddy was eating here that night when he got a phone call, telling him Señor Flame had hurt his knee and wouldn't be at the game. He thought it would be pretty funny to tell some of your gambling buddies, like it was a big tip or something."

"What gambling buddies?" protested Hathaway. "I gotta clean operation here. You hear that, Miss Ettenger?"

"Sure, sure. So Freddy gives this information to the boys at the bar, Charlie, and a few hours later someone borrows Señor Flame's uniform, short-circuits the Stadium, and shoots Lester Beldon in the back." The room fell silent; Sussman could tell he had spoken a little too loudly.

"Oh, yeah?" whispered Hathaway. "You sure about that, Suss?"

"Positive. Now look, Charlie, whoever killed Lester had to know about Señor Flame being injured, and my guess is they found out about it here. So try and think back a little, okay?''

Charlie Hathaway twisted the butt end of his cigar around the corner of his mouth. "Andy," he said, "do you know what four-thirty in the afternoon is around here?"

"It's Happy Hour."

"Right. And you think I can remember everyone who was in this place at Happy Hour, much less a Happy Hour two-and-a-half weeks ago? Hell, Andy, I can't even tell ya for sure that Freddy Granger was here, or that I was here."

"I know you were here, Charlie, you took one of Lester's extra tickets for the game, remember?"

"Yeah, yeah. I'll tell you what, Suss, why don't you ask Arnie? He was working that afternoon." Hathaway shouted in the direction of the bartender. "Hey, Arnie?"

Arnie looked up from the beer mugs he was swabbing.

"Arnie, you were working here the night Lester Beldon was murdered, right?"

"Yeah . . ." Arnie craned his neck to see who Charlie Hathaway was talking to. "What about it?"

"Mr. Sussman, here, thinks there was something suspicious going on. You remember Freddy Granger eating at the bar, saying something about Señor Flame not showing up for the game?"

"Nope," Arnie said quickly. He snapped the dishrag, squeezed it, and returned to swabbing the glasses. "Happy Hour, Charlie. Must be a hundred people coming in and out."

"You sure?" said Sussman, staring at Arnie.

The bartender glared at Sussman for a moment, then reached for the rinsing nozzle and sprayed hot water over the sudsy rack.

"Can we interpret that as a negative response, Charlie?"

Hathaway belched some cigar smoke toward Andy. "Listen, Suss, maybe you ought to try and get some more information."

"Mister Hathaway," rang a gravelly black voice.

Charlie jerked his head around. "Hey, Reddick old pal, whaddaya say!"

Sussman twisted backward and saw Dwayne Reddick stride in, looking like a walking advertisement for *Gentlemen's Quarterly*. He was dressed in earth-tone leather pants, a leather jacket, and shiny black cowboy boots. "Hiya, Dwayne," Sussman said.

"Andrew, what brings you to this part of the city on a Sunday afternoon?" Reddick placed a flat, rectangular package on the placemat. "And who's this beautiful young lady?"

"Dwayne, this is my attorney, Susan Ettenger. Susie, Dwayne Reddick."

"Ah, your attorney . . ." Reddick took Susie's hand gently in his massive palm. "It's a pleasure to meet you, Miss Ettenger. Andy's told me all about you."

"Is that right?" said Susie.

"Dwayne's studying to be a lawyer," Sussman said. "So, naturally, when the subject turns to law, he's interested in how other people make their way up through the legal profession."

"Of course."

"So," said Charlie Hathaway, extending a stubby hand towards Reddick, "to what do we owe the honor of this unexpected visit?"

Reddick tapped the package he had set on the table. "I thought this might be a good time to add the Reddick profile to Hathaway's Wall of Immortals."

"Hey, you brought the picture, Dwayne. Great!" Charlie's eyes lit up. "I've got just the place for it, too. Right over the bar, between Ernie Banks and Walter Payton."

"I'm truly honored," Reddick said, opening the package. "Now, why don't we have the signing ceremony? You got a bright red pen, Charlie? I want your patrons to be able to see through the haze, self-inflicted and otherwise."

"Just a second," said Hathaway. He trundled off toward the entrance alcove to get a pen.

"Hey, I like it," Sussman said, examining the framed, eight-by-ten-inch glossy. It showed Reddick standing just inside the front alcove at Hathaway's, wearing a Flames warm-up suit and autographing a basketball for one of the waitresses.

"Can I see it?" asked Susie.

Sussman started to show the picture to Susie, then pulled it back. "Hey, wait a second. Dwayne, take a look at this."

"What?"

"See this girl?" Sussman pointed to a slightly out-of-focus woman standing a few feet behind Reddick, just inside the door.

"Yeah. . . ."

"That's Sly's girlfriend, isn't it? You know, the one that's been following him around the last couple of weeks, keeps coming down to the locker room?"

Reddick held the picture to the light. "Yeah . . . yeah, I think you're right, Andy. Now that you mention it, she does look sort of familiar."

"Here we go," said Charlie Hathaway, returning with a bright red pen. "Scrawl your John Hancock with this, Dwayne."

"Charlie," said Sussman, "do you recognize this girl?"

Hathaway grabbed the picture and held it a few inches from the tip of his cigar. "Yeah, sure, I recognize that broad. That's Vicki Rogers. She used to be the hatcheck girl here.''

''That's it,'' said Reddick. ''I knew I'd seen her here.''

''The hatcheck girl,'' repeated Sussman. ''Charlie . . .'' He flashed back to his date with Wendy Altman. ''Charlie, weren't you complaining a few weeks ago about a hatcheck girl who walked out on you?''

''Yeah, that's the one. Damned broad didn't give me two weeks' notice or nothin'. Took me a month to break a new girl in, ended up costing me seven hats and a leather jacket. And then that son-of-a-bitch Thomas, he waltzes in and demands severance pay for her! You think that doesn't take nerve?''

''Well, you know Sly,'' said Reddick. ''His women are always pumping him for money.''

''*His* woman? You mean she was shacking up with him, too?''

''What do you mean, 'him, too'?'' Sussman asked.

''She ran off with that comedian,'' Hathaway said, ''that was her whole reason for leaving. Bobby Giordelli, or Fiorello, or whoever it was. He was supposed to have some guest shot on a talk show in Dayton, then they were going off to California. I guess the money wasn't rolling in as fast as they thought.''

''Wait a second. . . .'' Sussman thought back again to his first encounter with Hathaway after the murder. The argument with the man at the hatcheck counter . . . Charlie complaining about his hatcheck girl, who's run off with a comedian. And Giordelli, Fiorello, there was something familiar about that, too.

''I sent her last week's pay to Dayton,'' Charlie said. ''Not that she deserved it; it was just to get Thomas out of my hair.''

Bobby, thought Sussman. He had heard the girl mention a Bobby before, when she was arguing with Sly. Bobby

Giordelli? No. Fiorello? Sussman's mind shifted back to the collection of pictures in Shirley Beldon's basement. Bobby Fiorello, son of Lester's old teammate, Jimmy. The picture of the three of them . . . Lester being Bobby's godfather. "Charlie," Sussman said, "do you remember when this girl Vicki walked out on you?"

"Yeah," Hathaway growled. "I told you."

"I mean do you remember exactly when it was, in relation to the night Lester Beldon was murdered?"

Charlie thought for a moment. "It wasn't after, that's for sure. It was definitely before—maybe three, four days before."

"Was she in the bar that night, Charlie?"

"No. . . . No, I'm sure of that, Suss. I would've remembered."

"What about her boyfriend—this Bobby guy?"

"No, I'd have noticed him, too. Besides, he'd gone to Dayton, according to her."

"Hmm." Sussman took a sip of beer. "What about Sly? Did he show up, maybe in the afternoon? Was he around when Freddy Granger got his phone message?"

"Hard to remember," Hathaway said. "The guy usually causes a stir. Hey, Arnie!" The bartender turned around. "You remember if Sly Thomas was in here Lester Beldon's last night? In the afternoon, I mean, when Freddy Granger was here?"

Arnie considered the dirty glasses, then looked up. "Yeah," he said. Then, more convincingly, "Yeah, he was in here for a few minutes that night, come to think of it."

"Was he here when Freddy got his phone call?" Sussman asked.

Arnie shrugged. "I'm not sure. He might have been." He squeezed his washrag in the sink and went back to his dishes.

"The man has a keen sense of observation, Charlie."

"Sorry, Suss, best I can do. I'll buy your lunch, if it makes things any better."

"Thanks, Charlie, you're a real pal."

"I try and help out. I know you're not working."

"Right," said Sussman. He reached for his coat.

"Don't we get to stay for dessert?" Susie asked.

"Dessert?" said Hathaway.

"Dessert?" echoed Sussman. He could not recall ever hearing the word "dessert" uttered in Hathaway's Pub before.

"I just thought with a Sunday brunch we might get a little apple strudel, or devil's food cake."

Hathaway wiped a fat paw across his nose. "I gotta bag of Oreos in the kitchen," he said. "They're maybe getting stale, though."

"That's okay," said Sussman. He put his coat on and helped Susie out of her chair. "Maybe another time. So long, Dwayne."

"Later, Andrew. You comin' on the road trip next week?"

"I don't know, I hope so."

"Nice meeting you, Miss Ettenger," Dwayne said.

"The pleasure was mine."

"So long, Charlie," Sussman said. He and Susie buttoned their coats. They pulled on their hats, waved goodbye, and headed back out into the midday Chicago chill.

22

"COULDN'T YOU GET a better picture of Bobby Fiorello?" Murray asked, squinting at the faded newspaper clipping Sussman had cut from an old *Tribune* arts-and-entertainment section.

It was Tuesday afternoon, and Sussman had spent the better part of the day completing Murray's latest assignment, the results of which were pasted to the wall of Glick's office. "Best I could do," Sussman said, examining the row of photographs. "His picture's not exactly on every marquee in town, and I didn't want to steal the one off Shirley Beldon's rec-room wall. Besides, time's running short."

Time *was* running short. The Flames were playing their last game of the home stand tonight before embarking on a ten-day, seven-game road trip. If Sussman was going to have any chance of landing an announcing spot for this year's NCAA tournament, he would have to clear himself soon, preferably before the team left town.

"No sweat, Hoops," Murray said, inspecting the row of pictures at nose length: Fiorello, Sly Thomas, Arnie the bartender, Charlie Hathaway, Señor Flame. "Let's see here. Vicki Rogers . . ." Glick looked at the slightly out-of-focus clip that had been blown up from Dwayne Reddick's photograph. "Vicki worked as the hatcheck girl at

Charlie Hathaway's all during the time Lester was passing cocaine to our mysterious Mr. P.''

"The purchaser."

"Right. And we know Vicki was shacking up with Fiorello and that she also had something going with Sly Thomas. At least one of them *has* to have something to do with Lester's murder."

"I'll go that far with you, Murray."

"Let's assume it's Sly."

Sussman stood in front of Sly's picture, which he had cut out from the Flames' yearbook. "I don't know, Mur, I thought he was finished with that sort of thing."

"Sorry, Hoops, the evidence is right here." Murray pulled a cigar out of his canister, clipped the end off, and flicked on his VCR. The videotape monitor flickered on, showing a freeze frame of Lester Beldon interviewing Sly Thomas. "October twenty-seventh—this is the day the transactions started. Coincidentally, it's the day Sly Thomas returned to the team after a three-day absence during which he missed one game, allegedly to visit his sick mother." Murray released the freeze frame.

"Hi, there, everybody," Beldon was saying, "we're at halftime of tonight's game between the Flames and the Portlands, and we're happy to have our old pal Sly Thomas as our guest. Sly, welcome back! I understand your mother's been a little under the weather, lately."

"Oh yeah, Lester, my poor mama, she's really been fightin' it with that flu," said Sly. "Her temperature, it be up roun' one-hundred-ten degrees. The doctors spendin' days tryin' to figure out what's wrong."

Murray stopped the frame. "A hundred and ten degrees, the old lady's dead as a doornail, Hoops. And look . . ." Murray pointed to Sly's left hand. He seemed to be gesturing at something, or someone, on the side. "See that?" Murray started the tape again.

"She's been needin' personal attention and everything," Sly was saying. "That's why I had to go down to Georgia for a few days. I hate to miss a game just when we're comin' outta the gate, Lester, but you know how it is—when your mama needs you—"

Murray stopped the tape again and tapped the corner of the screen. "See," he said, as the camera pulled back a little. "Now look at the coat in the background." As Murray started the tape, the coat disappeared. He stopped the tape. "Sly wanted to be on hand for the first transaction, Andy, just to make sure everything went right." He continued with the tape.

"Fortunately, she's feelin' a lot better now."

"Well, that's just great, old buddy," said Lester Beldon. "I know *my* mother comes down with hay fever every now and then—"

"Murray, that's pretty flimsy evidence," Sussman said, as Glick turned off the tape.

"That's just the beginning, Hoops. I checked a few things out on my own. First of all, Sly's mother is in perfect health. Turns out she'd really like to see her son, Sylvester—it's been almost a year since he was home last. He hardly even phones her these days, except one time last October, when he called her real hush-hush"—Murray lit his cigar—"and told her that if anyone should happen to call after him, she was too sick to talk and he was off trying to get the doctor."

"I suppose you discussed all this with Mrs. Thomas?" Murray smiled. "She's a wonderful lady, Hoops. She figured it was all right to talk about it now, especially to Sly's old high-school coach."

"What a clever guy."

Murray leaned back in his swivel chair and puffed his cigar. "Hoops, it's obvious, isn't it? Sly takes off a few days to take care of his sick mother, only she's not sick, and he never visits her. The day he comes back, a cocaine transaction starts taking place. Sorry, pal; I know he's an entertaining guy, but he's up to his ass in this thing.''

"It's still hard to believe," Sussman said. "He tested clean, Murray. And what about Lester? How did he get involved in all this?''

"Money, Hoops. Pure and simple. Lester needed it. Sly could help him get it.''

"That's the one part of this whole thing I still don't buy, Murray—we don't have one shred of evidence that proves Lester had any financial difficulties.''

"Patience, Hoops. Let's just get through the scenario.'' Murray referred to a legal pad, which he had filled with a series of arrows and circles that looked like an advanced molecular theorem. "Sly agrees to set up a cocaine deal for Lester, but neither one wants to get anywhere near the exchange, for obvious reasons. So Sly gets this great idea: He's gotten friendly with Vicki Rogers, the hatcheck girl at Hathaway's, and he makes a deal with her. Lester'll come in every night before the game, as usual, and check his coat. Vicki has the coke: she closes the door to the hatcheck room, hangs up the 'back in five minutes' sign, and sews the toot into the coat lining. Later, while Lester's taping his interview, someone grabs the coat, opens the lining, takes the coke and replaces it with the money. Lester removes his share after the game, leaves the rest in the lining, and Vicki takes it out the next time around. She keeps her cut, gives Sly his, and everything's clean.'' Murray slid his chair back and propped his feet up on the desk.

"Sure, Murray, wonderful. *If* you accept the fact that Lester had a financial predicament.''

"Just wait, Andrew, I'll get to that. Now, we know that after the first few weeks someone started cutting the cocaine, right? And let's assume it wasn't Lester, because

Lester didn't know what was causing his rash. So let's figure it was Sly—and remember it was Sly who was making contact with Mr. P. Now, at some point Mr. P discovers his coke's being diluted—''

"Yeah, yeah," Sussman said. "And Sly blames it on Lester, and Mr. P rubs out Lester. But look, Murray, if Mr. P is some type of major-league drug dealer, don't you think he'd be more likely to have Lester taken for a ride somewhere and dumped in a car trunk, rather than planning that whole setup at the Stadium and dressing someone in Señor Flame's uniform?'' Sussman picked up Murray's newest lead-slug paperweight and juggled it in his hand. "And how would he know that Señor Flame was going to miss the game that night, Murray? How does that whole scheme fit in?''

"Well . . .'' Murray scratched his head. "Someone who was at Hathaway's that afternoon must have told him. You told me Sly was there, right, Hoops? Maybe he was helping Mr. P.''

"But that was according to what Arnie the bartender told *me,* Murray. And I'm not sure I believe Arnie.''

Murray got up slowly and returned to his row of pictures. "So check out Arnie's story. Go ask Freddy Granger. If Sly was there that night, Freddy'd remember it.''

"And if he wasn't?''

Murray stood in front of Arnie's picture. "Then Arnie's lying.'' He stared at Arnie's face, then at the fuzzy videotape blow-up of the man in the ski jacket. "Of course, Arnie's been around this whole transaction for months, he could have stumbled onto something. Maybe he was in on the action.''

"Sure, sure. And there's other questions, Murray. Why does Vicki keep hanging around Sly all this time? And why's she so worried about that testimonial for Lester tomorrow night?''

"I'm sure she has her reasons. Maybe she's upset because Lester's death stopped her cash flow. She probably never even knew Sly was cutting the coke."

"You're stretching, Murray."

"No, Hoops. Look, figure that her boyfriend Bobby's been having trouble getting his career off the ground. Money was scarce to begin with, and now Lester, his godfather, is dead. The drug money's dried up. Maybe Vicki thought she could bribe Sly. Maybe . . ." Murray stared at the row of pictures, then walked over to the smudgy print of Bobby Fiorello. "Wait. Hoops, what kind of act does this kid do?"

"I don't know. He's a comedian. And not a very good one, evidently."

"No, no." Murray took the clipping off the wall and read part of the article that was folded under it. "One-liners, gags, put-downs . . . here." Murray squinted at the article. "He does impressions. Hmm . . ."

"Murray, could we get back to Lester Beldon's alleged financial difficulties? This whole theory of yours hangs on that, and so far you've got zilch."

"Sure, sure . . ." Murray stuck the Fiorello clipping in his pocket. "All right, Hoops. We're almost there. Now I want you to go back to the Stadium tonight, okay?" He handed Sussman his coat.

"Tonight?"

"Before the game. Talk to Freddy Granger. Find out whether Sly was at Hathaway's the night in question."

"Oh, great. And where'll you be?"

Murray looked at his legal pad, then glanced up at the pictures on the wall. "I've got one more little experiment to run, then I should be ready to close this case out. By tomorrow, if we're lucky."

"You seem pretty confident, all of a sudden."

"You want everything settled before the team goes on the road, I assume?"

"That was the whole point, Murray. If we wait much longer, I can forget about the NCAAs this year."

"Well, then, let's get on it. We've got the rest of today, and tomorrow night's that memorial thing for Lester, right?"

"Right." Sussman grabbed his jacket. "Murray," he said, "are you really sure we can pull this thing off?"

"Hoops, I promise you, come Wednesday night we'll be drinking champagne and toasting the next Brent Musburger. Just get me that information."

"I'll work on it."

"Good." Murray Glick blew a smoke ring that floated towards the ceiling and wafted out into the mall. "Andrew," he said, "there's going to be one less picture hanging over Charlie Hathaway's bar after Wednesday night." He stared out at the row of pictures on his own wall, then escorted Sussman out of the office. "Maybe more than one."

23

ANDY SUSSMAN STOOD on the empty floor of the Stadium, musing about the hundreds of athletic events he had attended there over the years. It occurred to him that his moods, his friends, even his career, had become dependent on the outcome of the games that took place there. Not that Sussman was without self-esteem—he considered his reputation as the Flames' play-by-play man to be impressive, especially among hard-core basketball fans. But he couldn't deny that his general level of popularity fluctuated with the usually futile efforts of a group of overpaid, underachieving, and largely immature jocks—and now one overgrown delinquent, in particular, was threatening his whole career.

"Howya doin', Andy?" said Freddy Granger, spotting Sussman as he walked into the locker room. "You back on the job tonight?"

"Not yet, Freddy. Say, Fred—"

"Just a second. I gotta go talk to the coach, give him the injury report. I'll be right back."

"Wait," shouted Sussman as Granger headed for Weaver's office. "Freddy, is Sly around yet?"

"Yeah, he came in a few minutes ago. Today's complaints include a bad ankle, bad elbow, sore knee. He's in the sauna."

Sussman took off his overcoat and sat for a moment in Granger's empty office. Then he removed his cashmere sweater, sport shirt, T-shirt, and slacks, leaving himself naked except for his boxer shorts. He walked over to the sauna, where he heard a squeaky, out-of-tune voice warbling from inside.

"Lo-o-ove, babeee," sang the voice. "Comin' back home to meeee . . ." As Sussman entered the sauna, Sly Thomas dropped his hands and turned sideways. "Hey, Sustman, what you doin' here, man? You lookin' for interviews, you can catch me at courtside, no need to get your shorts all sweated up."

"Actually, Sly, I had this sudden yearning for a little dry heat." Sussman yanked the chain that hung above the pile of rocks. A burst of water whooshed out, sending a cloud of steam over Sly's face. "Sly, it's time we had ourselves a private talk."

"Sustman, baby, you gonna burn us up."

"Be cool, Sly." Sussman waved some steam from his eyes and stepped toward Thomas. "Sit down and make yourself comfortable. It's time we had a little discussion about Lester Beldon."

Sly Thomas took a step back toward the wall. "Whatta we need to discuss him for, Sustman, he's dead as a dodo."

"Maybe I should be more specific. We need to talk about Lester and your little cocaine deal."

"What're you talkin' about, Sustman! I ain't into no drugs, man, an' I don't know nothin' about Lester Beldon."

Sussman hit the steam chain again, flooding the room with a hot, white haze.

"Aack!" coughed Thomas.

"Think a little harder, Sly."

"I got nothin' to think about."

"I think you do." Sussman took another step toward Thomas, who slipped backward, caught his step, then stumbled into the double-tiered benches which were attached to the sauna walls. "Sly, last October you took a few days off to visit your poor, sick mother, remember? Only she wasn't sick, was she, and you never visited her. You used those days to score some cocaine."

"That's bullshit, Sustman! You ain't got nothin' on me."

"Patience, Sly. See how this sounds: You worked out a nice little deal with Lester and Vicki Rogers. Lester left his coat with Vicki at Hathaway's, Vicki sewed the coke into the lining, the switch was made before the games, everybody got a cut."

Sly Thomas scowled and sat sullenly on the lower bench.

"Sound familiar, Sly?"

"I ain't sayin'," Thomas said. " 'Sides, it's all over now. Lester's dead, it's too late to change anything."

"Too late for Lester, maybe, but not too late for me. Now I want some information, Sly, and fast."

"You can shove that, Sustman."

Sussman hit the chain again. The steam was beginning to get into his own lungs, but he could see that Sly was sweating much more profusely. "Whose idea was it to cut the cocaine, Sly? What's the matter, you weren't making enough profit for your three days' work? A couple of hundred thousand dollars wasn't enough?"

"I don't know what you're talkin' about, man."

"Don't bullshit me, Sly. I know why Lester was killed. Poor guy got in over his head, didn't realize he couldn't trust you."

"What're you *talkin'* about, man? Whatta you mean, 'cuttin' the cocaine'? I didn't cut nothin'. I didn' have nothin' to do with that product, 'cept gettin' it in the first place." Sly caught himself in midsentence and slumped back on the bench.

"Right, Sly. . . ." Sussman opened the sauna door a crack and let some of the steam seep out. "Sly, look at me and tell me you didn't know that cocaine was being cut."

"I don't know nothin' about that."

Sussman hit the chain again.

"Sustman, I ain't jivin'."

"Sly, I want to know who shot Lester Beldon. I want to know why Lester needed the money in the first place. I want to know who else was in on that deal. And I want to know who the buyer at the other end was."

Sly wiped some sweat off his face. "How about we discuss this over a beer, Sustman? I know a nice little place on Rush Street. We can meet after the game."

Sussman reached for the chain.

"Hey!" Sly started for the door, but Sussman blocked his path. "Listen, man—first of all, I don't know what Lester Beldon's problems were. He says to help him with a deal, I don't ask questions. If someone was cuttin' the toot, I don't know anything about that either, understand? Once it leaves my hands, I got nothin' but the cash, and that be gone a long time ago. Maybe Lester Beldon was cuttin' the stuff himself."

Sussman shook his head slowly. "Sorry, Sly. Lester never knew the product was being tampered with, you can trust me on that. So who's left? Your friend Vicki? And what about her boyfriend, Bobby? And who was that buyer, Sly?"

Sly turned sideways again. "Listen, Sustman, you take my advice, you just sit back, let this whole thing blow right on by. Nobody's got a thing on you, we both know that. Maybe you did somethin' to piss off your people at that radio station, or at the po-lice. Maybe they like to see you sweat for a while, but they'll back off in time. You get your job back pretty soon, next year at the latest, maybe get a nice little settlement.''

"Sorry, Sly, I don't think that's going to be adequate."

"Then you take that job in Indi'napolis I told you about! What's wrong with that, Sustman? You get a fresh start—''

"Sly," said Andy, "you know what?"

"What?"

"I don't think I want to start a new career in Indianapolis. I just don't think it's my kind of town, know what I mean?''

"Hey, man, you'll get used to it."

"No, Sly. No, I don't think I could ever get used to Indianapolis. I think I'm just going to have to ask around a little more." Sussman opened the sauna door. "And you know, Sly, your buyer, whoever he is, he might not be too pleased to find out that he killed the wrong man. He might feel real guilty about that." Sussman took one step out of the sauna. "He might want to find out who the real cheat is, Sly.''

"Sustman, wait!" Sly bolted from the bench. "Listen, man, I had nothin' to do with cuttin' that cocaine, understand, so I ain't no cheat. They got no reason to go after me.''

"I guess that's a matter of interpretation. Of course, if you want to help me with the explanations—''

"There ain't no explanations!" Sly's voice slipped into a high-pitched squeak. "Sustman, look—fat ol' Lester's gone now, I can't bring him back. You ain't never gonna find the dudes that killed him.'' Sly tried to yank Andy back inside the sauna, but his arm slipped, and Sussman stepped back into the chilly locker room.

"Hey, Freddy," shouted Sussman, catching a towel Granger had thrown him.

"In a minute," Granger said. "Some guy's here to fix the whirlpool, I gotta sign for it."

Sussman hopped over the wet floor toward Granger. "Wait, Freddy, just one question. Remember the night Lester was killed, you had dinner at Hathaway's?"

"Yeah."

"Try and remember. Was Sly Thomas around when you got the phone call about Señor Flame?"

"Sly? Of course not, Andy. Coach Weaver doesn't want any players in that place on game days. There's gamblers hangin' around, ya know, league regulations."

"You're sure?"

"Positive." Granger tossed Sussman another towel and headed for the whirlpool. "Dry off, Andy, there's a flu goin' around."

"Hey, Sustman," shouted Sly, who was still standing at the sauna door. "You listen to me!" He stumbled down toward Andy. "You keep quiet about this, understand? You make too much noise, more innocent folks gonna get hurt."

"Well, Sly, we sure wouldn't want that to happen, now, would we?" Sussman toweled off and pulled his shirt on.

"Sustman, wait."

"Conversation's over, Sly. If you've got more for me, let me know."

"There ain't no more!"

Andy Sussman finished dressing silently as Sly Thomas glared at him.

"Sustman, you be careful. You watch what you be sayin'."

"Have a nice game, Sly." Andy Sussman smiled and dried the last bit of moisture off his face. "See you in the box scores." Sussman tossed his towel away. He grabbed his parka and pulled on his hat. Then he waved good-bye to Sly and marched out of the locker room.

24

AT FIVE O'CLOCK on Wednesday evening, two hours before the memorial dinner for Lester Beldon was scheduled to begin at Hathaway's, Andy Sussman walked into Murray Glick's Northbrook Court office and found it empty, save for Peggy the receptionist.

"I was out for coffee when he left," Peggy said, munching on a croissant. "I think he left an envelope for you on his desk." She hit a button behind her telephone, buzzing open the door to Murray's inner office. "You can walk right in; just don't open the cabinets or anything, they're all wired."

"Right." Sussman had agreed last night to meet Murray here and drive downtown with him—a last opportunity to review the evidence before going public with whatever case they had. Apparently, Murray still had some last-minute business to clear up.

Sussman walked into his office, noticing immediately that the photographs had all been taken down, along with the assortment of false mustaches and caps Murray had stuck on them last night. He had been trying to match one of the suspects with the mysterious man in the ski jacket, but had succeeded only in making the pictures impossible to identify at all. Sussman searched Murray's desk and found the envelope. "Hoops," the note read. "We're almost there—I just need an hour or so to mix the frosting. Got to fly, meet you at Hathaway's, 7 P.M.—MG."

Sussman parked his Datsun at a garage on Dearborn Street and slogged his way along the sidewalk toward Hathaway's Pub. The Loop seemed like a dismal place to him on winter nights such as this, when the Chicago sky was dark by five o'clock and the only stars visible were not stars at all, but the glimmers of high-rise buildings several blocks away. Sussman had no immediate plans for it, but he hoped that if a memorial were ever held for him, they'd find a nice deli in Highland Park, or maybe one of the chic new restaurants uptown—at least some place with a good salad bar.

"Hello, Andy," said Shirley Beldon, greeting Sussman as he stepped under Hathaway's frayed canopy. She was greeting all the guests as they entered, as well as a few wayward strangers looking for a quick drink, who were gently steered away by Charlie Hathaway. "I'm so glad you could make it. It's sort of our last chance to get everybody together and say good-bye to Lester. I'm sure he would have wanted you to be here."

"I wouldn't dream of missing it," said Sussman, kissing Shirley on the cheek. He walked into the restaurant and looked around for Murray.

"Hiya, Suss," said Charlie Hathaway, stepping out of a shadow and slapping Sussman on the back. "Howya doin' tonight?"

"Just fine, Charlie." Sussman thought Charlie looked more than a little harried; deep furrows had appeared on his forehead and chin, perhaps at the prospect of serving a legitimate dinner to over a hundred people.

"Well then, how about wettin' the old whistle?"

"Scotch and water would be nice, Charlie."

"At your service."

"Andy, my man, good to see you!" Sussman turned

and saw Dwayne Reddick towering over him, along with a tall, striking black woman he introduced as Vonetta. "You all by your lonesome tonight?" Reddick asked, wiping a few specks of dirt off Sussman's lapel. "What happened to that beautiful attorney friend of yours?"

"She's supposed to be here later on, Dwayne, if she can get away from the office. I'm not her only case, unfortunately. Are you two part of the official entourage?"

"We're emissaries of good will from the Chicago Professional Basketball Club, Incorporated. I think they wanted a few people they could depend on not to pass out halfway through the dinner." Reddick waved his hand out over the crowded restaurant. "The coach is here, plus Jack Bryce and Freddy Granger."

Sussman looked around the room. Because of the predominance of basketball people, he had to stand on his tiptoes to see who else was in attendance. "Dwayne," he said, "is that Sly?"

Reddick cupped his right hand above his eyes and peered across the room. "Well, I'll be damned. Look at that, Andy."

Sussman squinted through the cigar and cigarette smoke. Sly Thomas was standing in a corner, dressed in a gray suit and sunglasses. He was nursing a drink and gazing, trancelike, at some of the pictures on the wall.

"Sly doesn't seem his old, jovial self today," Reddick observed.

"No, he doesn't, does he?"

"Here you go, Suss," said Charlie Hathaway, handing Sussman a Scotch and water. "Drink up, I think we're gonna start the dinner pretty soon." Charlie sneaked a glance at his watch. "Why don't you folks grab a table, maybe the others'll follow suit—the stuff's gonna get cold if I leave it sit around much longer."

"Excuse me," said a waitress, walking past with a tray filled with dinner salads.

"Salads? Is this a new look, Charlie?"

"I hired some guy to do the catering," explained Hathaway. "Nobody here can cook anything but hamburgers."

"Lester never ate anything but hamburgers."

"Well, I was expecting a classy crowd. Hey, isn't that your boss over at 'CGO? Grant, or whoever he is?"

"Wilfred P. Brandt. Yeah, Charlie, that's him."

Hathaway stirred the swizzle stick in Sussman's drink. "Hey, who knows, Andy, they like the meal, maybe they'll come back." He waved at another one of the guests and started to edge back into the crowd. "Enjoy, folks. I gotta get people in their seats."

Sussman turned and looked at the tables, which had been arranged to form a wide semicircle, with a makeshift dais at the center. He picked out one that was off to one side and a few rows back and took a seat next to Dwayne and Vonetta, leaving an empty chair for Murray and another for Susie, if she came.

"Good evening, Andy," said Wilfred P. Brandt, stopping by the table with his wife. He was dressed in a dark blue suit with a small Chicago city flag pinned on the lapel. "Glad to see you could make it; I know it means a lot to Shirley. Incidentally, have you met my wife?"

Sussman had met Brandt's wife several times, briefly, at the station's annual Christmas party, where she had always shaken his hand firmly and wished him a happy Hanukkah.

"Alice, this is Andy Sussman, one of our announcers—he's on a little vacation right now."

Sussman did his best to engage Mrs. Brandt in some small talk, then breathed a sigh of relief as he saw Susie Ettenger walk in. She was being escorted by Murray Glick. "Excuse me," Sussman said, "I think my, uh, date's here.'' He pushed himself away from the table and headed toward the doorway, where Murray was exchanging greetings with Shirley Beldon. They seemed to be having an animated conversation, for two people who had ostensibly never met before.

As Sussman approached, Murray whispered something into Shirley's ear, then patted her on the shoulder and directed her back into the crowd. ''Hoops!'' he said, sidling closer to Susie.

''Well, if it isn't the mystery couple,'' said Sussman, searching Susie's face for a hint of a smile. She looked piqued and was clutching her purse like a baseball bat.

''Sorry, pal,'' Murray said, slipping his arm around Susie's waist. ''Didn't mean to break your heart, but you know how it goes. A chance meeting, some idle conversation, a little champagne—*ouch!*'' He grabbed his belt, which had just absorbed a direct hit from Susie's purse.

''Hi, Suse,'' Andy said. He helped her with her coat. ''Rough day, huh?''

''Just the last twenty minutes,'' Susie said icily.

''I think I'd like to sit down,'' Murray said, rubbing the indentation his belt buckle had made in his stomach. ''Andy, you got us a table?''

''Over there, Mur, with Dwayne Reddick and his girl-friend. Susie, could you keep our seats warm for a minute? Murray and I need to have a little talk.''

''That's okay, Andrew. Susie's all cued in.''

''Actually,'' said Susie, ''I'd like to get something in my stomach. I haven't had anything to eat all day except some crackers and a cup of yogurt.'' She took off a woolen scarf and gave it to Sussman, then whispered in his ear, ''I swear, Andy, if that guy touches me one more time—''

''Try and relax, Suse.''

"Hoops," said Murray, as Susie walked away, "I think you've got the inside track on that girl."

"Murray . . ." Sussman looked around to make sure no one was listening. "Murray, what the hell's going on around here? What'd you do with the pictures?"

"Just a little last-minute detective work." Murray surveyed the restaurant. "Where's Arnie the bartender? Is he on duty tonight?"

Sussman looked over at the bar. Arnie, who had been tinkering with the dishwasher, popped his head back over the bar top. "He's right there. Hey, Murray, what was going on with you and Shirley Beldon?"

"Where's Bobby Fiorello?" Murray looked over at the dais. "Ah, there he is, right next to Shirley."

Sussman followed Murray's stare. Fiorello looked slightly taller than he had in the picture. He was slim, almost gaunt, with dark, wavy hair, plastered back in a style reminiscent of the fifties.

"That takes care of everyone but Sly," Murray said, edging Sussman toward their table.

"I think he's hiding somewhere in a corner. I haven't seen Miss Vicki, though."

"I don't think Miss Vicki's exactly a friend of the family." Murray stepped back, barely avoiding a waitress carrying a tray of soup bowls. "She's here, though."

"Where?"

"Take my word for it, she'll show up." Glick, his camel's hair overcoat slung over his arm, led Sussman back to their table. "Hi, folks," he said. "Sorry I'm late. I'm Murray Glick. . . ."

Sussman introduced Murray to Dwayne and his girl-friend, then sat down, noticing that his half-eaten salad had been moved over one spot, allowing Susie to sit in his original chair. She was now sandwiched between him and

Vonetta and out of Murray's reach, although she still had to look at him.

"Hey, Murray," Sussman whispered, as a waitress took away the salad bowls and served a main portion, which appeared to be some type of chicken dish, "where's Señor Flame?"

"Strained his knee in practice again. Don't worry, Hoops, he checks out."

"You sure?"

"Eat your dinner. The fun doesn't start 'til after dessert."

Sussman shrugged and ate his dinner, joining in the light conversation and sneaking occasional glances at Sly Thomas, who spent the whole meal slouched over a bar stool, sipping beer from a bottle. About halfway through dessert, Sussman heard the sound of a butter knife tapping against a water glass; the room fell silent as Charlie Hathaway stood up to speak.

"Good evening, everybody," Charlie said, to a smattering of applause, "I'm glad everyone could make it. As you all know, tonight we're honoring the memory of our old and dear friend, Lester Beldon. Lester was a regular here. . . ." Charlie reached for a glass and sipped some water. "That is to say, he was one of our most frequent and honored guests, so I think it's appropriate that we're hosting this little ceremony." Hathaway put his cigar down and introduced Shirley Beldon, who stood up meekly and waved to the crowd. He stumbled through a few more sentences, then called on Wilfred P. Brandt to begin the ceremonies.

"Always a pleasure to listen to old W.P.," Sussman said to Murray, as light applause filtered through the room. "Is the show going according to plan?"

"Patience, Hoops."

"Good evening." Wilfred P. Brandt coughed and addressed the audience in the plodding monotone he reserved for public engagements. "It's with a great deal of sadness that I approach this task tonight. Lester Beldon was a much beloved member of the WCGO family. If viewer response means anything, and I believe it does—"

"Jesus Christ, he's reading his eulogy again," Sussman whispered.

Brandt droned on for about half an hour, presenting a summary of Lester Beldon's career from his high-school days all the way through his years as "one of the NBA's premier television and radio analysts," then mercifully yielded the floor back to Hathaway. There followed a number of cameo appearances by team members: Ted Weaver telling about long plane trips when Lester had mixed gin-rummy games with coaching tips; Jack Bryce on how Lester had influenced his development as a "top-flight NBA center." Dwayne Reddick on what a "fine gentleman and inspiration" he was.

"Aren't you going to say anything, Hoops?" Murray asked, scouring the roll basket for one last Rye Crisp.

"Are you kidding? C'mon, Murray."

"It might make Mr. Brandt feel a little more kindly to you when all this blows over. The man's dead, after all; you wouldn't want to be the only one who didn't say anything."

"And now," said Charlie Hathaway as Reddick sat down, "I'm sure we'd like to hear a few words from Lester's closest professional associate, our old pal, the Voice of the Flames . . ."

"What in the hell—"

"I was just trying to give you a little advance warning."

"Andy Sussman, c'mon up here," said Hathaway, as the dinner guests applauded.

Sussman left his seat and headed slowly for the dais, trying to think of something appropriate to say. As he reached the microphone, he saw Murray excuse himself and head for the men's room. "Ahem," Sussman began, keeping an eye peeled on the back of the room. "I guess I knew Lester as well as anybody—when you work with a guy every night for three years, it's almost like he becomes part of your family . . ." Sussman fumbled with his tie, trying to recall some anecdotes that would evoke pleasant memories of Lester. He settled on a story, slightly embellished, about a blizzard in Cleveland that had left them marooned in the back of a bus, playing gin rummy until three in the morning, when the National Guard finally cleared a path to the airport. As he was finishing, Sussman glanced toward the men's room. The door swung open and Murry walked out. "I guess I may have had a little fun at Lester's expense over the years," Sussman concluded, pausing as Murray stopped behind Freddy Granger on his way back to the table and whispered something in his ear. "But all I can say is that it was an honor to know him, and I'm sure I'll never be able to work again without remembering his influence." Sussman, feeling like he had been standing at the dais for an eternity, walked back to a smattering of applause.

"Nice speech, Hoopsie," said Murray, tapping his heart. "Hit me right here. That showed a lot of class, buddy."

"Murray, what's going on? The show's almost over."

"Stay on your toes, Andrew."

"Ladies and gentlemen," Charlie Hathaway said. "I'd like to introduce a special guest now. This gentleman had a lifelong association with Lester: His father, Jimmy Fiorello, was one of Lester's teammates with the old Cincinnati Royals, and when little Bobby, here, was born, Lester became his godfather." The audience applauded. "And if that wasn't enough, when young Bobby decided to go into show business, Lester was right there to help. Lester got

Bobby's career started with a gig right here in town, and we're happy to announce that Bobby's just taped an appearance on 'The Larry Miller Show,' which'll be airing next April seventeenth. Bobby, we've brought in a keyboard here for you—how about doing a few numbers for us? Ladies and gentlemen, how about a warm welcome for Bobby Fiorello!''

Bobby Fiorello pulled his lanky frame from the table and walked to the dais. He wavered behind the small, portable electronic keyboard and, in a voice that was apparently supposed to sound like John Wayne's, said, ''Well, good evening, pilgrims.''

''Now?'' said Sussman, as the crowd applauded politely.

''Soon,'' said Murray.

Fiorello tickled the keys with a few light jazz chords, then looked up and spoke in his own voice. ''I wasn't exactly sure what to do tonight, ladies and gentlemen. I know it's a somber occasion, but I thought maybe I'd do a couple of the things that Lester used to get a kick out of. . . .'' He resumed his pattering on the keyboard and looked nervously at the audience. ''Here's Jimmy Stewart. . . .'' He lapsed into a passable Jimmy Stewart imitation. ''Jimmy Stewart, doing the Beatles' 'With a Little Help From My Friends.' '' A few titters rose from the crowd as Fiorello impersonated Stewart singing the Beatles' song. ''Thank you, thank you. Here's another one that Lester liked. . . .''

Back at the table, Murray had turned around so that he was staring at the door to the kitchen.

''Murray, what're you looking for?'' asked Sussman, wincing at Fiorello's awful impersonations.

''Shh.''

At the dais, Fiorello lifted a Scotch glass and let out a large belch. ''Ladies and gentlemen, this is what I think

W.C. Fields might have sounded like, reading the Gettysburg Address." He took a gulp of Scotch. "Ah yesssss, four score and seven years ago-o-o-o . . ."

"Hey, Bobby," shouted Freddy Granger, interrupting the act, "you wanna do a request for us?"

"Request?" Fiorello looked blankly at the rows of tables.

"C'mon, Bobby, you know the one I mean."

Murray tapped Sussman on the shoulder. "Here we go, Hoops."

Fiorello waved some smoke out of his eyes. "Uh, I don't know, Freddy, what kind of request?"

At the dais, Shirley Beldon twisted and stared at Murray.

"C'mon, Bobby," Granger insisted, "do Lester for us."

"Lester?" An uneasy rumble swept across the room. Fiorello, his hands clamped to the edges of the keyboard, looked nervously down the dais. "I'm not sure that's appropriate, Freddy."

"Aw, come on," Granger said. "Hey, folks, Bobby used to come downstairs after the game and do this great impersonation of Lester. I swear, we thought someone had the radio going."

"Freddy—"

Fiorello turned sideways and looked at Shirley, who had stopped staring at Murray and was now whispering something to a man sitting beside her. "Go ahead, Bobby," she said weakly, glancing again at Murray.

Fiorello shrugged. "Okay," he said, clearing his throat. "Just a few words, though." He tinkered nervously with the piano. "Ahem . . ." He breathed loudly into the microphone to simulate crowd noise. "It's halftime, folks, and we're happy to—"

"Get down, Bobby!" shouted Murray Glick, vaulting out of his chair as a gunshot rang out from the back of the

room. A bullet ricocheted off the podium as Bobby Fiorello dropped safely underneath the dais.

"Andy!" shouted Susie Ettenger, her scream joining those of a hundred other people.

Sussman grabbed Susie and dived under the table. A second gunshot rattled across the room, but Sussman, his perception jolted, could not determine its source. "Murray?" he shouted to the bottom of the table. He lay on the floor, his body shielding Susie's, listening first to the shouting of the other guests, then to silence as people waited for further activity. "Murray?" He looked down at the tangled layer of legs that stretched across the floor. He was expecting Murray to join them any second, but Glick stood rigidly in front of the table.

A few more seconds of silence followed, then the creaking of chairs being pushed aside from somewhere near the kitchen. *"Freeze!"* shouted Murray Glick. Sussman heard the click of a trigger being cocked above his head. "Hold it right there."

"All right, all right already," shouted a female voice. "Keep your pants on."

"Just keep those hands up, sweetheart, it's all over." There was another brief silence, then Sussman heard the door open, and the floor echoed with the hard soles of a dozen of Chicago's finest. A moment later, Murray ducked his head underneath the table. "Wake up, lovers, the ride's over."

Sussman helped Susie up, then stared at Murray, who was holding a revolver. Across the room was a division of policemen, led by Detective Lafferty. One of the cops was holding a red-haired woman, her wig pulled halfway off, dressed in a waitress's uniform. It was Vicki Rogers. She had been grazed in the right hand—just enough to dislodge her gun, which Lafferty now held in a handkerchief. Another policeman was fastening a pair of handcuffs around Arnie the bartender. A third was apprehending Bobby Fiorello.

Murray Glick slipped the safety on his gun and placed it on the table. "Ladies and gentlemen," he said, "I'd hate to end the party prematurely." He paused as the remaining guests got off the floor. "I just thought you might like to hear one more story before you go home." He waited to see if any objections were forthcoming; there were none. "Once upon a time," he began, "there was a little boy who wanted to make oodles of money—more money than he'd ever made before, which was no small amount to begin with."

Back at the bar, Sly Thomas had broken out in a cold sweat. His right hand was in his pocket, fondling what may or may not have been a gun. In any case, Murray had his eye on Sly, and Sly was frozen in Murray's stare.

"Now, out of pure humanitarianism," Murray continued, "we won't publicly announce who this person was, since he isn't the one responsible for our little gathering tonight. But I'm sure he won't object to me letting you know about this ingenious plan."

Sly took his hand out of his pocket. He ordered another beer and slumped back on his bar stool.

"It seems that our friend got involved in a cocaine deal," Murray said, "a half-million dollars profit, free and clean. Getting the product was no problem; all he had to do was find a buyer, arrange a discreet transaction, then sit back and collect rent. The only problem was, our friend happens to work in a very sensitive profession—drugwise, that is. His employers didn't trust him to begin with; they were watching him ver-r-r-y closely to make sure he didn't get involved in transactions *just like this one.*" Murray sipped on some water. "So our friend thought, What I need is a front. Someone so unlikely to be involved in a drug deal that no one would ever suspect him. And who, ladies and gentlemen, could be a more unlikely prospect than Lester Beldon?''

A gasp swept across the room.

"Surprised?" said Murray. "Not as surprised as I was. Not as surprised as my friend Andy Sussman was. Andy was accused of being involved in Lester's murder, and as much as he wanted to clear his name, even *he* didn't believe Lester could be involved with drugs. But . . . the person who would have been *most* surprised about Lester Beldon selling cocaine never found out about it in the first place. He never had any idea what was happening to him, not even as he was being shot in the back. Right, Bobby?''

Bobby Fiorello stared at the floor.

"Come on, Bobby, you want to try that impersonation of Lester for us again? The police are here, no one's going to shoot at you this time.''

"I just thought it was a one-time deal," Fiorello mumbled. "I didn't know they were going to kill him.''

"Of course you didn't, Bobby. But when the stakes are half-a-million dollars, accidents can happen, can't they?'' Murray turned back toward the rows of tables. "Well, folks, on with the story. Our friend—we'll call him Mr. X for now—had a great idea. Why not have someone *pretend* to be Lester Beldon. Why not have someone contact the purchasers, say they were Lester, and arrange the whole deal, without Mr. X ever meeting them, or ever talking to them, or touching anything except the money. And what a perfect team he had available! Bobby Fiorello, who could impersonate Lester perfectly; and Bobby's girlfriend Vicki Rogers, who was the hatcheck girl at this restaurant.''

Back at his table, Andy Sussman was sipping some coffee, listening as Murray described the cocaine transfers just as they had discussed it in his office. The only embellishments came when Murray got around to Arnie the bartender.

"Our team had clear sailing," Murray explained, "until one day Arnie, here, suspected some funny business and walked into the coatroom just as Miss Vicki was doing some lining-repair work. Miss Vicki got out of that crisis easily enough: she cut Arnie in for a percentage. But the portions are all a little smaller now, and Vicki begins to think, 'Hey, I'm in the driver's seat.' She's got custody of the product, after all, and she dispenses the earnings. So she starts tampering with the coke, cutting it with powdered borax. Not much, but then again, it doesn't take much. Those extra few grams she keeps for herself are worth a nice piece of change each, right Vicki?"

Vicki glowered at Murray, but did not appear to have anything to add to the narrative.

"Now," said Murray, "here's where things began to get tricky. Miss Vicki figured she could cut the coke for a couple of weeks, then split town before anybody was the wiser. But the people she was playing with weren't amateurs. A couple of weeks after the dilution started, Bobby Fiorello called the buyers to confirm another pickup, and they had some very threatening things to say to him. Such as how about a discount on the next payment, turkey, and stop tampering with the product, or else Bobby—or Lester Beldon, as the buyer was led to believe—would end up under an expressway somewhere."

Fiorello, his hands cuffed behind his back, stared at his patent-leather boots.

"Now, sports fans, our little team of business people begins to panic. What if, they thought, the buyers weren't satisfied with the settlement? What if someone gets sent to deal with Lester directly? What if, in fact, they find out that it really isn't Lester at all they've been dealing with?

Things could get extremely hot for Vicki, Bobby, and Arnie, that's what.

"On the other hand, what if Lester should suddenly die, violently, with no apparent provocation? The buyers will figure that Lester was double-dealing and someone did their job for them. The police will never be able to figure out who did it, and if some innocent persons have to sweat it out for a while, that's just their tough luck. And best of all, Vicki and Bobby and Arnie will be home free, with money in their pockets.

"There's only one trouble, though: Bobby's had enough. He doesn't want any part of a murder, especially when the victim is his godfather. He says 'no way' and goes off to Dayton to do his show. But Vicki, Vicki knows something has to be done. She quits her job at Hathaway's and gets ready to go on the lam. She and Arnie make preliminary plans for the power blackout." Murray turned to Detective Lafferty. "I think that part of the crime has been researched quite adequately, right, Detective Lafferty?"

Lafferty nodded. "It was a small explosive device. Security wasn't very tight—it could have been stuck in there before the game, or during the game. The suspect's been taking electronics courses at IIT for over a year now. It would have been well within his knowledge."

"So Vicki had things all arranged," Murray continued. "No messy ambushes or bodies to dispose of. She'd do it right there at the Stadium, in the dark. All she needed was a foolproof opportunity to commit the murder undetected—and luckily enough for her, it came sooner than expected."

Murray took a long draw from a bottle of beer and continued. "Because one fateful afternoon, February fifteenth to be exact, Freddy Granger comes into Hathaway's and gets a phone call, which he shares with the boys at the bar. It seems that Señor Flame, the team mascot, is in the hospital and won't be at the game that night. Arnie the bartender hears this and has an inspiration. He calls up Vicki. A few hours later, Lester comes into Hathaway's for his pregame drink and, per his custom, leaves a few extra tickets at the bar. Arnie sticks two of them in his pocket.''

Murray surveyed the crowd at Hathaway's. Not a soul was stirring; the only sound was the dishwasher at the bar, going through a rinse cycle. ''Before Lester leaves,'' Murray continued, ''Arnie arranges a fake phone call for him, supposedly from a sponsor who wants to have dinner after the game. Arnie figures Lester will call Shirley and tell her to stay home—that's important, because Shirley sits at the game with binoculars, staring straight at Lester. She might see something, even if it's dark. Lester falls for the bait, and a few hours later, Vicki and Arnie go to work. Arnie's job is to take care of the blackout; Vicki's is to pull the trigger, but she has a few things to do first. She has to be in disguise even before she gets to the Stadium, so she can sneak into the locker room. So she dresses herself in worker's overalls, tucks her hair under a stocking cap, and sticks on a phony mustache.''

Murray turned to Sussman. ''That was the last part of the puzzle, Hoops. See, I really hadn't figured Vicki as our man in the ski jacket. Then, last night, I put the photocopy away and looked at the videotape directly, in color. I noticed the red hair, then took Vicki's picture back out . . .''

Murray turned his attention back to the audience. ''Ladies and gentlemen, a few minutes before the end of halftime, Vicki Rogers left her seat and walked downstairs. While the players and coaches were heading back to the floor for the second half, she sneaked into the locker room; that left her a half hour to find Señor Flame's locker, open it, and put on his uniform. After that, she was home free—the security guards didn't know Señor Flame was hurt, they wouldn't do anything to stop her once she was in costume.'' Murray paused to look Vicki Rogers directly in the eye. Vicki scowled at him, turned around, and faced the bar. "At nine-fifteen, dressed in the mascot suit, Vicki Rogers entered the floor area and started dancing behind the press table. At nine-sixteen the explosive charged, and the Stadium blacked out. At nine-sixteen and thirty seconds, Vicki Rogers pulled a gun out of her pocket, the silencer screwed on. She unzipped Señor Flame's costume, aimed squarely at Lester Beldon's back and shot him dead. By the time the power was restored, she'd returned the costume, put her ski jacket back on, and was walking out of the Stadium.''

Inside Hathaway's Pub the audience was deathly quiet, their eyes alternating between Murray Glick and Vicki Rogers.

"Don't feel too bad, Vicki,'' Murray said, "it almost worked. You just got a little careless, that's all. A little borax powder spilled here, some messy sewing in the lining there . . . and how could you have known about Lester's rash?''

Back at the bar, Vicki Rogers fidgeted in her handcuffs. She twisted backward, making a pointed effort to ignore Murray.

"Murder's an intricate business, isn't it, Vicki?'' continued Murray, smirking in self-satisfaction. "All that time, all that planning, and you never know where the slip'll come, do you? That one little detail, that one piece of bad luck—''

"Oh, stuff it, Sherlock!'' said Vicki. She kicked the side of the bar, knocking several glasses over, and jabbed a policeman with her elbow, sending him stumbling toward the door. "Come on, let's get out of here,'' she said to the cop. "I don't need to listen to some two-bit gum-shoe gloating all night. Get me out of this firetrap, you can read all about it in the papers tomorrow."

Murray shrugged. "No need to be a poor sport." He flicked the safety of his revolver on and stuck it back in his pocket. He finished his beer and reached for a stray bread stick as the policemen spirited Vicki, Arnie, and Bobby Fiorello out the door.

Within a half hour, Hathaway's Pub had emptied out. Shirley Beldon had been escorted home by Wilfred Brandt and his wife, the players and coaches had filed out as unobtrusively as possible. Charlie, his bartender suddenly unavailable, was anchored behind the bar, washing glasses and settling up with the caterers. Andy Sussman, Murray Glick, and Susie Ettenger were standing by a small table in the back, buttoning their jackets.

"Well, Hoops, are you satisfied?" Murray brushed some crumbs from a packet of Rye Crisps off his pants. "Everything signed, sealed, and delivered by tournament time, just as promised."

"Murray, you've done a commendable job." Sussman wrapped his right arm around Susie Ettenger. "So what do you think, Suse? Is Murray Glick an okay human being, or what?"

Susie folded her arms and considered the question. " 'Okay,' yes," she said, after a few seconds. " 'Human being,' I'm not so sure."

"Well, that's a step in the right direction," said Murray. "Hey, listen, you two, here's a great idea. Wendy Altman got four tickets for the symphony tomorrow night. Maybe we could double-date. Meet for drinks, go out for dinner, see the symphony—what do you think, Suse?"

Susie's face took on a look of extreme disgust. "Andy," she said, "it's getting late. Maybe we'd better go, before my judgment gets impaired too much."

"We could always forget the drinks," Murray said.

"Murray," said Sussman, "I think possibly Susie needs a few days to digest the situation. Maybe have a couple of private meetings with her client to tie up business? Right, Suse?"

"No offense, Murray," said Susie. "I thought Andy and I just might spend a quiet evening by ourselves this weekend. Maybe some other time."

"Hey, no problem. Fact is, I could never stand that music anyway." Murray removed his Russian hat from his coat sleeve and set it on his head. "Fact is, I was just thinking that it's getting late and I haven't slept much the last few nights. It might be time for old Mur to move along." He rubbed Susie on the back and kissed her hand. "So long, sweetheart."

Susie jerked her hand away and wiped it on the tablecloth.

"Later, Murray," Sussman said, trying to position his body between Susie and a butter knife. "Thanks for everything." He grabbed the knife and tossed it onto the next table.

"So long, Hoops," said Murray, winking at Sussman.

Sussman winked back. He kissed Susie softly on the cheek as his friend ambled out the door.

25

THE BOEING 727 taxied down the runway at O'Hare International Airport and prepared for its departure, carrying Andy Sussman to his first network sports assignment. Sussman mused that boarding a 6:15 A.M. Great Plains Airways jet to Lawrence, Kansas, was not the image he had associated with the words "network sports," but that was where the first round of the NCAA subregional was being played, and he was not complaining. Just getting the opportunity for network exposure was a tribute not only to the influence of his friend Danny Borenstein in New York, but to the negotiating skills of Susie Ettenger. The regional was taking place the same night as a Flames game, and the management at WCGO could not understand why Andy was so eager to renege on his contract, considering that he had gone to such lengths to try and have it enforced. Susie, in reply, had casually mentioned to Wilfred P. Brandt that her client had already been grievously misused, was still a victim of vicious innuendo and could suffer additional damage to his career if he was not allowed to take advantage of this opportunity.

Susie, as it happened, had begun to take a much greater interest in Sussman's career since the conclusion of the case. The idea of Andy flying around the country as a network play-by-play announcer did not turn out to be as unsettling to her as he had feared. She had been working twelve-hour days at the law firm for over a year now, working through Saturdays and holidays and vacations; the prospect of a boy-friend working for CBS Sports, she had informed Sussman, did not seem like such a terrible thing. Susie had even mentioned the possibility of quitting the law firm altogether and becoming Andy's agent. It was food for thought.

Sussman pulled out his *Chicago Tribune* and scanned the headlines. He usually went straight for the sports section, but the Lester Beldon murder indictments were still going on, and he had been enjoying the daily reports. Vicki Rogers, to no one's surprise, had become the main target of the prosecutors. Bobby Fiorello, who had not killed anyone or tried to, had agreed to turn state's evidence in return for immunity. He would be given a new name and background; with his ability to pick up dialects, he would probably survive wherever he was relocated. Arnie, mean-while, had pleaded guilty to a conspiracy charge instead of murder, in return for testimony against Vicki. She was being tried for first-degree murder, and by the looks of things, the state had built a pretty solid case against her.

Sussman put the front page down and turned to the sports section. The Flames, according to one of the columnists, would be looking for a new point guard in the upcoming draft, due to the unexpected illness which seemed to have ended the career of Sly Thomas. Sly, Sussman knew, had somehow managed to avoid being fingered by any of his co-conspirators, at least for the time being. The prosecutors had agreed not to press charges against him, in return for a signed deposition which would be used only if the state's case against Vicki Rogers ran into difficulty. There was no guarantee, of course, that Vicki Rogers would remain silent forever, and Sly had come to the conclusion that, given the circumstances, it would be best to suspend his career for the duration of the season and resume it in a different locale. He had mentioned that Barcelona, Spain, might be a suitable place.

"Now, you listen, Sustman," Sly had said, as he cleared his belongings out of the Flames' locker room. "You be readin' those international newspapers, you hear me? I be tearin' up that European League. You look for the box scores from Barcelona." Sly whispered in Sussman's ear. "Wali Azoul-Hazam. Can you remember that, Sustman?"

"Wali Azoul-Hazam? Can *you* remember that, Sly?" Sussman did not think so. In any case, he hoped that Sly Thomas would spend the off-season working on his jump shot. He could imagine some high-rolling Chicago Mafioso scanning the European basketball box scores, stopping at the line:

Azoul-Hazam—FG 3–13, FT 2–11, 1 Assist, 8 Pts, 5 Fouls and saying, "Vito, I think that's our man."

As Sussman opened the inside of the sports section, a note slipped out and fluttered into his lap. It was from Murray, who had driven him to the airport. Murray had continued to go out with Wendy Altman for several weeks after the case had been solved, finally breaking off the relationship after Wendy had bought two tickets to the New Zealand Shakespeare Festival, complete with airline and hotel package, and charged it to his American Express card. Sussman read the note:

Hoops: It occurred to me, as I was in the shower this morning, that I have been to Lawrence, Kansas, previously. It was a case I worked on back in the Highwood days, alienation of affection, if I remember correctly. It so happens that I made a friend there. Not, I would say, a lasting friend, or one who would be likely to mix in with my present clientele, but a worthy human being, nonetheless. I didn't think it was worth a long discussion, but I wanted to give you the benefit of my travels. If you get bored, her name is Cheri and her number is 938–9932. If you can't reach her there, try any of the lounges at the Best Westerns. Have fun and get the names right. Murray.

Sussman balled the note up and stuffed it in the ashtray by his right hand.

"Can I get you some coffee?" asked a stewardess, rolling a cart past his seat.

"A Bloody Mary would be nice," Sussman said. Stretching his arms as the plane took off, he made a mental note to phone Susie the minute he reached the motel in Lawrence. The thought inspired him to open up his wallet and look at a small picture of her; it was a passport photo, taken so she could monitor a probate hearing next month in Costa Rica. Smiling, Sussman admired the photo for a few minutes, then closed the wallet and tilted the seat back as far as it could go. He closed his eyes, thinking of the soft bed he had abandoned at his Lincoln Park condo, thinking of Susie, thinking of the cramped, lonely motel room that would be awaiting him in Lawrence. Don't complain, he told himself—this is what you wanted.

Sussman, alert now to the day that was beginning below him, looked out the window and watched the sun rising over the cornfields. Somewhere in Kansas, he knew, a bunch of twenty-year-olds were waking up with butterflies in their stomachs, worried about the game that he was covering on CBS tonight. Twelve hours to get ready, Andy thought. He took out the press kit that had arrived by courier the night before and turned to the team rosters. Time to get to work. As the plane winged its way across the prairies, Andy Sussman flicked on his overhead light. He covered one side of the rosters with his hand and began memorizing the names and numbers of the players who would be competing that night.